★ STAR PATTERNS ★

"Earl!" whispered Navalok. "Earl, look at the ceiling!"

Dumarest shifted his eyes and froze, stunned by what he saw.

The winking points of brilliance shining by the reflected light of the torch, points which vanished even as he studied them. Impatiently he moved a little, the points shining clear again as the beam of the flashlight hit and was reflected from the rayed disc.

"Patterns," said Navalok wonderingly. "They make patterns, Earl. But of what?"

Of stars. Of the Zodiac. Of the constellations seen from Earth.

Here, in this place, could lie the clue which would guide him home!

SPECTRUM OF A

FORGOTTEN SUN

E. C. Tubb

DAW BOOKS, INC.

DONALD A. WOLLHEIM, PUBLISHER

1301 Avenue of the Americas
New York, N. Y.   10019

DEDICATION

To Ken and Pamela Bulmer

FIRST PRINTING, NOVEMBER 1976

1 2 3 4 5 6 7 8 9

PRINTED IN U.S.A.

Chapter One

On Hoghan a man lay dying. He sprawled beneath the jagged stump of a broken tree, blood puddling the dirt around his hips, the uniform he wore ripped and torn, burned and stained. In the flame-shot darkness his voice was a tormented whisper.

"Earl?"

"Here." Dumarest knelt, feeling the squelch of mud, reaching out with his left hand to grip the other's shoulder. "Relax, Clar. You'll be all right."

"Don't lie to me, Earl." The pain-wracked voice held a bitter impatience. "Am I a raw recruit to believe a thing like that? I'm as good as dead and you know it. That laser caught me right across the guts. If I hadn't been armored I'd be dead now." The voice drew strength from pain and anger. "Damn the armor! Damn it! Damn it all to hell!"

A flare rose from a point close to hand, cold, blue-white light throwing stark shadows from the ruined buildings, the broken remains of once-decorative trees. Once the city had been a gentle place graced with statues and things of beauty; now the fury of internecine war had turned it into a shambles.

"Earl!" Clar writhed beneath Dumarest's hand. "The pain! Dear God, the pain!"

"Easy!"

"I'm burning! My guts—!" The voice became an animal-cry of searing agony. A shriek which could bring unwanted attention.

With his free hand Dumarest tore at his belt, jerking open the pouch it contained, spilling free the contents. An ampoule tipped with a hollow needle rose to bury itself in the writhing man's throat. A pressure and numbing drugs laced the bloodstream. A temporary measure only; nothing available could heal the wound. In the blazing light of the drifting flare Dumarest examined it.

The armor Clar had worn, like his own, was cheap stuff, protection against low-velocity missiles, falling debris, shrapnel and ricochets. It could even give some defence against the glancing beam of a laser, melting even as it distributed the heat, but the beam which had caught Clar had been directly aimed and the plate across his stomach had flared like paper, adding molten droplets to the searing energy of the blast. Beneath the twisted metal and charred clothing the flesh was burned, black and red with char and blood, the greasy ropes of exposed intestines bulging, perforated, crisp with cauterised tissue.

"Earl?" Calmed by the drug Clar's voice was flat and dull. "It's bad?"

"Bad enough."

"I knew it." A hand rose to push the helmet from the sweating face, thin grey hair accentuating the age-lines now prominent at eyes and mouth. "A hell of a way to end. Ten years with the Corps and never a wound and now it's the end of the line. Well, it happens. A man can't live forever, Earl."

But no man had to die like a beast in the mud of a city, spilling his guts for the sake of another's ambition. From somewhere came the roar of an explosion, the rattle of small-arms fire. Flame, red and leaping, rose to dull the watching stars, the distant points of brilliance cold, remote, hostile in their indifference.

"Listen," said Clar. "Hide out until it's over. Pick a spot and crawl into it and stay there until its safe to show yourself. Wait until well past dawn and, when you move, keep your hands open and high. You understand?"

Beneath his fingers Dumarest could feel the growing acceleration of the pulse in the dying man's throat.

"Be smart, Earl. Learn from one who knows. So we've lost, so what? There'll be a penalty to pay, but later, when cool, the winners will listen to reason. Now they'll kill anything moving on sight. I. . . ." His voice broke, returning edged with pain. "A burn like that—why is it taking so long?"

The weapon itself had seen to that, cauterising the flesh and preventing the swift loss of blood which would have brought a speedy and merciful end. An irony. In another time and place the man could have been saved, frozen, placed in an amniotic tank, the ruined tissue replaced with other grown from his own cells. Now he could only wait for death.

"Earl?"

"I'm here, Clar." Dumarest tightened his hand. "My fingers, can you feel them?"

"Yes, but I can't see you. Everything's gone dark." In the light of the flare the eyes rolled, wide, the balls mottled with red. "You're a good man, Earl. The kind a man needs at his side when he goes into battle. But the life of a mercenary isn't for you. You're too smart. Too clever. Take my advice, Earl. Get out while you can. Don't waste your life. Don't— God, Earl! The pain! The pain!"

More drugs would do nothing but stave off the inevitable and the toxins flooding the man's bloodstream diminished their effectiveness. But it was all he had. Dumarest used three more of the ampoules then snarled as Clar heaved beneath his hand. Old stock or diluted contents; someone, somewhere, had made an easy profit and because of it a man would die in screaming agony.

"Earl!"

Dumarest moved his hand, the fingers searching for the carotids, finding them, pressing deep to cut off the blood supply to the brain. Unconsciousness came almost at once but, as Clar relaxed, he maintained his grip. To allow the man to wake required a sadistic bent he did not possess. It was kinder to be merciful. More gentle to kill.

The tide of battle had moved to the south, gunfire echoing from the area of warehouses huddled close to the field, flames rising from burning houses, some lurid with the writhing colors of fuming chemicals. Swathes of green and orange, darts of blue and amber, a golden haze shot with the searing brilliance of burning magnesium which obliviated the need of flares and sent shadows dancing over the torn street and shattered buildings. An eruption of violence wasteful in its extravagance for, as he knew, the battle was over, the victory assured to the other side. But war did not have a tidy ending and armed men, fearful of their lives, would take no chances.

As his hand fell from the dead man's throat Dumarest heard the scuff of a boot, a sharp, metallic sound, and was moving as gunfire tore the air and missiles threw gouts of dirt from where he had knelt.

"Captain! I've got one! Here!"

The gun fired again as Dumarest rolled, the man holding it too excited to take careful aim. Bullets sprayed the ground, one tearing at the heel of a boot, another ripping through armor to graze a shoulder, the impact like the kick of a horse.

"Captain!"

Dumarest felt the jar of his helmet against stone and flung himself behind a sheltering mass of fallen debris, moving towards the end as bullets sent chips whining through the air. From cover he peered up and outwards, seeing the figure silhouetted against the lambent glow. A man, young from the sound of his voice, wearing the black and maroon of the opposing forces, a sub-machine gun cradled in his arms. A raw recruit on his first mission, forgetting elementary precautions in his excited desire to kill. A veteran would have taken cover, aimed with care, counted his shots, and Dumarest would now be dead. Instead the fool stood in full view, firing wildly, the gun falling silent as the magazine exhausted itself.

As he reloaded Dumarest rose, his own gun lifting, leveling, his finger checking on the trigger as a deep voice called from one side.

"Lorne! Down, you fool! Down!"

To fire now would be to betray his position, to invite answering fire from the man who had called. A veteran, this, knowing better than to show himself, one who would not miss.

"Captain! He's over there! Behind that stone!"

"Down, you fool! Hit the dirt!"

"But—"

"I'm using a grenade."

It exploded in a blossom of flame as Dumarest dived for the cover he had spotted, a narrow crack in a shattered wall, shrapnel whining inches from his helmet, dust stinging his eyes as he dropped to turn and stare into the flame-lit darkness. Two men at least, but the captain would not be alone, with him would probably be a patrol sent to sweep up any stragglers and, when they found no body, they would close in.

Dumarest looked upwards. The crack narrowed as it rose,

to climb it would merely place him in a blind extension of the trap in which he was placed. Behind him reared a jumble of debris, stone precariously balanced which would fall if he attempted to burrow into it. The only way out was the way he had come.

"Lorne, check the area," ordered the deep voice. "And hurry!"

"One dead, Captain. He's the man the one I saw was trying to rob."

"Anything else?"

Boots scrabbled over stone and Dumarest heard the sound of ragged breathing as the young man came to investigate. A dark patch showed against the illuminated sky, light reflected from a pair of eyes, more catching a polished spot on the helmet. A target impossible to miss, but to fire would bring another grenade.

"Lorne?"

"Nothing, Captain." The young voice echoed its disappointment. "But he couldn't have got away. I'm sure I hit him and he couldn't have escaped the blast."

"Then he must be there. Look again."

The dark shape came closer, head bent, gun ready to fire. The finger on the trigger would be tense, a word, a movement and he would shoot without thought or hesitation.

Dumarest rose slowly, taking care not to touch the stone to either side. Lifting his gun he waited until the dark shape had turned away then threw it with the full power of his arm. It landed with a clatter, a sound immediately drowned in the roar of the weapon cradled in the mercenary's arms. A blast of thunder which sent echoes from the buildings and masked the thud of Dumarest's boots as he lunged forward. One hand lifted, weighed with his knife, steel gleaming, it came to a halt as it touched the bare face beneath the helmet. His other hand slammed over a shoulder to clamp over the chest and pull the body of the soldier hard against his own.

"Move and you die!" he snapped. Then, raising his voice, called, "I've got your man, Captain. Fire and you kill us both."

"Lorne?"

The man gulped as he felt the prick of the knife in the soft flesh beneath his chin.

"Answer him," said Dumarest, and dug the blade a little deeper.

"He's got me." The young voice was sullen. "A knife at my throat."

"Kill him and you burn," rasped the captain. "What do you want?"

"To live."

"You're surrendering?" The captain rose, his shape bulky against the sky. Others rose with him, four men all with weapons aimed. "Why didn't you call out before?"

"And be blasted by a trigger-happy fool?" Dumarest eased the pressure on the knife a little. "He gave me no chance. He fired as soon as he saw me—if he was my man I'd have something to say about him missing the way he did."

"He's young," said the captain. "And new—but he'll learn." He stepped forward lifting his helmet, revealing a hard face seamed and puckered with old scars. "Let him go."

"When he drops his gun."

"He won't shoot you." Reaching out the captain took the weapon. "But I may if given cause. Lorne?"

"He was robbing the dead," snapped the young man. As Dumarest released his grip Lorne stepped forward, turning to rub his throat, looking at the blood staining his hand. "A ghoul," he said bitterly. "A damned ghoul."

"He was a comrade," said Dumarest flatly. "And I wasn't robbing him. Stop trying to justify yourself, youngster. And while you're at it you can thank the captain for saving your life. If he hadn't called out you'd be dead now."

"You—"

"That's enough, Lorne!" The captain turned to where one of the others rose from his examination of the dead man. "Sheel?"

"He's got money on him. A wound in the guts and drugs are scattered around. My guess is that he was passed out easy."

"A comrade, eh?"

"Yes," said Dumarest. "And a good one. What happens now?"

The captain shrugged. "The engagement's over and you're among the vanquished. The orders were to kill all stragglers, but what the hell? You're worth more to us alive and you've earned your chance. Lorne, escort him to camp." He added, grimly, "And make sure that nothing happens to him on the way."

The room was like many others he had seen before. A bleak place with Spartan furnishings: a desk, a chair behind it, another facing it, set squarely on the floor and fitted with invisible electronic devices to winnow the truth from lies. A place designed to intimidate, holding nothing to distract the attention, as much a cell as the one in which he had been held since his surrender three days ago. Time which Dumarest had spent with the tireless patience of an animal knowing there was nothing else he could do.

Major Kan Lofoten was waiting for him. Like the room, he was the product of functional intent. Neatly uniformed in black and maroon, his face was a hard combination of lines and planes. His eyes, deep-set beneath slanting brows, were shrewdly direct. A man of middle-age, dark hair brushed back from a high forehead, his mouth thin and cruel. When he spoke his voice held an unexpected resonance, a depth of inflection which Dumarest guessed was as cultivated as his exterior.

"Be seated, my friend. Rest your hands on the arms of the chair. Relax, no harm will come to you. To business, but first my apologies for the delay. As you can imagine we have been busy." And then, without change of tone, he said, "You are Earl Dumarest. A mercenary attached to Haiten's Corps. Your first engagement?"

"Yes."

"You joined, where?"

"On Ragould." There was no point in lying and the man would already know the answer to the questions he asked. But he wanted more than bare answers. "I was desperate," added Dumarest. "I'd traveled Low and found no work available. The Corps was recruiting and it seemed a good idea to sign up. We left the next day and came to Hoghan. The rest you know."

"Perhaps." The Major moved some papers. "You have fought as a mercenary before?"

"No."

"But you have fought?"

"When I had to, yes."

Lofoten nodded and leaned back in his chair his eyes studying the figure before him. Tall, hard, the face edging

on bleakness. A man who had learned early to rely on no
one but himself. Stripped of armor and uniform he wore the
clothes he had carried beneath, pants and tunic of dull,
neutral grey, boots which rose to just below the knee. The
tunic had a high collar and long sleeves falling to mid-
thigh. One shoulder was scarred by the impact of a grazing
bullet, the glint of protective metal showing beneath the tear.
Only one thing was missing from his usual attire—the knife
which now rested on the desk before the interrogator.

Lofoten picked it up, turning it so as to allow the light
to glimmer along the blade. Nine inches of honed steel, the
edge curved, the back sweeping down to form a needle-
point. The guard was scarred and the hilt worn. Striking it
on the desk he listened to the clear note from the vibrating
metal.

"A good knife," he said casually, "but an unusual weapon
for a mercenary to carry. As unusual as the fact that you
wore your own clothes beneath the armor. Why did you do
that?"

"I didn't like what I was given."

"Cheap stuff, thin, tearing at a touch." Lofoten smiled, a
brief flicker of the lips which revealed a flash of white teeth.
"And your weapons the same, yes? How many veterans did
your contingent hold? What rations did you carry? How
were your logistics? How well were you officered?"

"Badly," said Dumarest and added, dryly, "as you must
know."

"Yes, I know, as you must have realised by now, that
Haiten's Corps was sacrificed. You had no hope of winning
and there was no intention that you should. It was nothing
more than a show. Sound and fury and some limited destruction, enough to awe the civilians and make them obedient
to the new regime."

"A show," said Dumarest bitterly. "But some good men
died."

"Of course—but dead men draw no pay." Lofoten was
cynical. "And who ever claimed that the life of a mercenary was easy? You realise why I'm telling you this? Your
Command has no interest in redeeming you. Unless you
have money to buy your freedom you are ours to dispose of
as we see fit. The penalty the vanquished must pay. Either
you work off your debt by service in the Legion or we sell
you as contract-labor. You have money?"

"No."

"Of course not, else you would not have joined up with Haiten on—where did you join?"

"Ragould."

"And you arrived there from where?"

"Elmish."

"And before that?" Too many worlds scattered across the spread of the galaxy. Names which had become faded memories, the habitats of people who were now ghosts. A fact Lofoten sensed. "Never mind. Just tell me the world of your origin." He blinked at the answer. "Earth?"

"Earth."

"A most unusual name for a world." Lofoten glanced at the desk, at the tell-tales relaying their signals. "Earth? I've never heard of it, but no matter, I am more interested in your future than your past. Incidentally Captain Sigiua was most impressed by your conduct. He has agreed to take you under his command should you join us. The captain was the one who had you sent to camp."

"I remember," said Dumarest. "If I did join you for how long would it be?"

"Things are slow at the present. Your expenses would be high and your income small. Even with rapid promotion, and I think that could be promised, it would take several years to gain your freedom. Then, of course, you could remain as a free-lance. Many men have made a career in a mercenary band and you could be one of them. Atlmar's Legion is always in need of good men and the rewards could be high."

And death could come fast with the burn of a laser, the shocking impact of a bullet, the blast of explosives. Dumarest thought of Clar and how he had died—a small return for a decade of loyalty, but a man would be a fool to hope for more. A bigger fool to join an organisation which traded in war and used harsh discipline to maintain its dominance over those wearing its colors. And yet had he any choice?

Leaning back Dumarest veiled his eyes and studied the bland face of the interrogator. It was a mask of tissue, tiny muscular reactions firmly controlled, the eyes like glass, the lips carved as if from stone. A proud face belonging to a proud man and once, perhaps, a sensitive one. An ambitious man, certainly, no other would have risen as high in the calling he had chosen to follow.

Lofoten's hands fell, toyed with the knife as, casually, he said, "A small matter which you can easily put at rest. You were crouched over the body of your comrade when discovered and were immediately fired on. Yet you escaped injury. How?"

"Luck," said Dumarest. "I heard the soldier and he fired without taking aim. The type of gun he was using throws up and to the right after the first shot."

"And so you moved down and to the left?" Lofoten shook his head. "No, my friend, I think there must be another explanation."

His hands moved on the knife and, without warning, he threw it from where he sat. An awkward position, but his aim was true and, spinning, the blade hurtled directly towards Dumarest. Lofoten drew in his breath as it slammed its point deep into the back of the chair, his eyes judging distance, the time allowed for intent to be recognised and evasive action taken. A normal man, anticipating the throw, would have barely been able to leave the chair. Dumarest stood three feet to one side of it, poised, watchful.

"Fast!" said Lofoten. "Never have I seen anyone move with such speed. As I suspected you possess an unusual attribute; the ability to evaluate a situation and take appropriate action on an instinctive level. And your reflexes are amazingly fast. No wonder the soldier missed. Well, that is one mystery solved. Now to another. Why did you join the Corps?"

"I've told you that."

"Yes, you said you were desperate," mused Lofoten. "But you could have earned money in the ring. Your speed and undoubted skill with a knife would have provided food and comfort. Not the need for money, then, but for some other reason. The desire to forget a woman? I doubt it. The urge to see new worlds? A remote possibility. The need to escape? Many seek sanctuary in a mercenary band. For a man hunted by assassins such a move could be wise."

Dumarest turned without comment and jerked the knife from the chair. For a moment he held it in his hand and then, as Lofoten made no objection, slipped it into his boot.

"Ragould is a small world with little shipping," said the major thoughtfully. "Which is why Haiten recruited there.

On such worlds there are always restless young men eager to travel and careless as to the true cost of their passage. But you are no star-struck fool and must have known the risk involved. Yet, for a man without money and with the desire to remain unnoticed, the opportunity would hold an attraction. A chance to disappear. One engagement and then, with pay and perhaps some loot, to move on to some other world. And, if any were following you, they would think you had died in the war."

The man was shrewd and had come too close to the truth for comfort. Dumarest was uneasily conscious of the days he had been held, an unnecessary delay unless time had been needed for investigations to be made. And beneath the bland words was something else, the hint of knowledge owned but not displayed, hidden like the whip of a trainer after its initial display.

He said, flatly, "Have you decided?"

"On what is to be done with you?" Lofoten bared his teeth in a flickering smile. "You will, of course, be sold to the one who bids highest for your contract. A pity you have no money—I have the feeling that the bids will be high and the possibility of you ever being able to regain your freedom remote."

Not remote, impossible should he fall into the wrong hands. A fact the major was making clear even as he hinted at a way out.

"I don't like to see a man of your calibre wasted, but it is the system and the rules must be followed. Of course, if you could raise the money, then as one soldier to another, I would be pleased to accept it."

"Give me two days and I will raise the money," said Dumarest. "That is a promise."

"One which, unfortunately, I cannot accept. The regulations must be followed you understand." Lofoten frowned and picked up a paper from his desk and then, as if remembering something, let it fall. It had been in clear view for a moment only, but long enough for Dumarest to see the symbol stamped on the heading, the hatedly familiar Seal of the Cyclan.

"I was forgetting," said the major. "A small matter which could be a fortunate coincidence. I have an aquaintance, a woman who is in some slight difficulty. It could be that you may be able to help her. She, of course, could help you in turn. Will you give me your word that you will make no attempt to escape if I send you to her?" He added, casually, "You will, of course, be under guard."

An opportunity he couldn't refuse. Trapped, Dumarest knew that he had no real choice, but caution made him reluctant to appear too eager.

"This woman, who and what is she? What would be my duties?"

"That she will tell you."

"And my pay?"

"To leave Hoghan," said Lofoten. His voice, his face, were expressionless. "To escape a rather difficult situation. Surely that is reward enough?" Then, smiling, he added dryly, "But there could be more. The Lady Dephine is a most unusual person."

Chapter Two

She was tall with a mane of auburn hair, and seeing her as she stood before the window, Dumarest felt a momentary shock of recognition.

Kalin?

Then she turned and he saw her face and eyes, green as Kalin's had been, but the similarity ended there. The hair lacked the inbred flame of the woman he had once known and the face was not the same. It was older and bore the stamp of a harsh determination, a feral intentness accentuated by the concavity of the cheeks beneath prominent bone. The mouth was wide, the lips full, parted a little now to reveal the predatory curve of sharp, white teeth.

She said, sharply, "You know me?"

"No, my lady."

"Your eyes. I thought—but never mind." To the guard standing behind Dumarest she snapped, "Wait outside."

"Madam, my orders—"

"Were surely not to insult me. Now do as I say." As the door closed behind the man she smiled and extended her hand. "Earl Dumarest. From what I hear you are something unusual. I'm glad of that. In a universe of mediocrity how refreshing it is to find the unique. Do you know what all this is about?"

"You are to tell me."

"Yes, of course. Well, sit down and take things easy while you may. Some wine?"

The room was in a hotel close to the field, a place of luxury untouched by the recent conflict. Only the ruins far to one side told of what had happened. As she busied herself with a bottle and glasses, Dumarest, ignoring the invitation to sit, crossed to the window and looked outside. It was close to dusk, the sun touching the horizon, yet activity had not diminished. Uniformed men guided and controlled traffic and pedestrians; gangs of workers cleared rubble and demolished shattered structures. They worked hard; within a few more days the city would be almost back to normal. Within a few months new buildings would have replaced the old, fresh trees taking the place of those now standing like shattered teeth.

"To the victor the spoils," said the woman at his side, where she had come to stand. Her voice was deep, almost masculine, rendered truly feminine by its musical resonance. "Look at them, Earl. Children playing with their toys. Bangs and noises in the night, the sight of flame, the trembling of the ground. Then, when it's all over, they come out of their holes and wave flags and chant songs of triumph. And they call it war."

"And you, my lady?"

"Stupidity." She handed him one of the two glasses she carried. The wine it contained was a lambent green holding the flavor and odor of mint. "Men are such fools. What has the war decided? That taxes shall be paid to one faction instead of another and to gain this so-called victory, what has it cost? A year's revenue at least to pay for the mercenaries. Two more to repair the damage. Wanton extravagance when the whole matter could have been settled by cutting a deck of cards."

Dumarest said, "An easy solution, my lady."

"Too easy, which is why they never take it. Always they need to strut and adopt their postures, make the same old threats and the same old appeals. Always they need sacrifice and blood. And always, they prate of their pride. Why are men such fools?"

"To have pride?" Dumarest sipped his wine. "Some men have little else."

"And so, because of that, it becomes more important to them than life itself. Is that what you are telling me, Earl? That a man is nothing without his pride? That rules dictated by others should determine how he should live and die? That tradition has the right to eliminate self-determination?"

Her voice had deepened, holding the raw edge of anger and acid contempt. Dumarest wondered why . . . not because of what she saw through the window. Earthquakes could ruin houses, and many cultures adopted a common garb, so destruction and soldiers were not unique to war. There were no dead lying in the streets, no blood staining the walls, no fragments of limbs and shattered tissue to tell of recent events. Like all mercenary-fought wars the engagement had been conducted with due consideration to those who footed the bill.

He said, casually, "If you had your way, my lady, some of us would find it hard to find employment."

"I was forgetting." Light flashed as she lifted her hand, each nail a silver mirror. "Yet how many soldiers actually kill? And what, to them, does killing mean? The touch of a finger can launch a missile to destroy a city a hundred miles distant. A child could do it, and children do. Children in uniform. Soldiers."

Dumarest watched as she poured herself more wine. Beneath the shimmering fabric of her high-necked gown her figure held the lithe grace of a feline. Her breasts, high and firm, were taut beneath the fabric above a cinctured waist, the long skirt falling over neatly rounded hips and thighs. A woman who carried little excessive fat, one whose metabolism would burn up energy as fast as it was ingested. One of indeterminate age, not young, but far from old. One, he guessed, who had lived hard and fast—as if to crowd two lifetimes into one. And she had the ingrained arrogance of a person born to the power and privilege of wealth.

Lowering the glass she met his eyes. Bluntly she said, "Well, Earl, do you like what you see?"

"Is that important, my lady?"

"No, but something else is. When you first entered this room I was watching your reflection in the window. You thought you recognised me. Correct?"

"You reminded me of someone."

"A woman?" She didn't wait for an answer. "It would have to be a woman. One with red hair, obviously, but redder than mine?" Her hand lifted to touch it and again light threw brilliance from her nails. Splintered reflections from metal inserts each honed to a razor edge and needle point. Talons Dumarest had seen before tipping the fingers of harlots plying an ancient trade. "Earl?" She was insistent. "What was her name? The woman I reminded you of, what was her name?"

"I've forgotten." A lie—he would never forget; but the subject was a dangerous one. Quickly he changed it. "I was

told that you could ransom me if I agreed to help you. The
guard is waiting."

"Let him wait."

"For how long, my lady?"

"Until I have decided. Until you have agreed."

"Agreed to what?"

She smiled and shook her head, a tress of hair falling
to veil one eye, a strand which she lifted and replaced
among the rest.

"My lady!"

"Why be so impatient, Earl? What waits for you if you
leave this room? Do you prefer a cell? And afterwards the
auction block and a life of contract-slavery? Or to be taken
and hidden away and used by those who are not known to
be gentle?"

The Cyclan? But if she knew of their interest in him then
why not mention the name? A guess, he decided. Neither she
nor the major was sure. The display of their seal had been
a goad or a calculated stimulus to gauge his reaction. An
old trick of any interrogator. Let slip a hint and then follow
up; probing, using the information the victim lets fall to
gain more. But what was the real connection between them?
Why had he been sent to the woman?

"To help me," she said, when bluntly he asked the question. "And to help yourself at the same time."

"How?"

She stepped towards him, arms lifting to embrace him,
her lips settling close to his ear. Her voice was low, a bare
murmur, impossible to hear from outside or to be caught by
any electronic device.

"To steal, Earl. To snatch the loot of a world."

From high to one side a man yelled. His shout drowned
in the rasp and rumble of falling rubble, the pound of a
pneumatic hammer thudding like a monstrous heart accom-
panying the snarling whine of a saw. Noise which filled the
air with blurring distortions as dust veiled sharp detail.

The day had died and night reigned but still work continued under the glow of floodlights. A uniformed figure
snarled a curse, then stiffened to salute as an officer barked
his displeasure.

"Sorry sir, but these civilians—"

"Are our employers." The officer, young, a neat dressing

on his forehead covering a minor wound, smiled at the woman at Dumarest's side. "Your forgiveness, my lady, but the man is fatigued. Battle tires a man and the war was a hard one." His hand rose to touch the dressing. "Even so he should have remembered his manners."

"You are forgiven, Captain." Her smile was radiant. "Your wound is not too serious, I hope?"

"I was lucky," he said modestly. "And medical aid was at hand."

"I'm glad of that. Well, goodnight, Captain. Perhaps we shall meet again. You are on duty here at night? I shall remember it."

"Captain Pring, my lady." His salute was from the parade ground. "If you need help be free to ask."

"A fool," she said as they moved on. "A typical soldier, Earl. A mannikin to be manipulated as if it were a stuffed toy."

Dumarest stepped over a low pile of rubble. "Why don't you like mercenaries?"

"Isn't it obvious? They come and fight their stupid war and then make out they have done their employers a favor."

"And haven't they?" He smiled as he halted and turned to face her; a man taking a walk with an attractive woman, a couple engaged in idle conversation. In the darkness eyes could be anywhere. "Think of the alternative. Without mercenaries you'd need to train and equip your own forces with all the expense that entails. Those who died would be close; sons, fathers, brothers, sisters even. And those engaged in civil war tend to ignore restraints and so increase the destruction. All the employers of mercenary bands really lose is money. It is strangers who do the dying."

"Not strangers to each other, Earl," she said pointedly. "Comrades. Is it easy to kill a friend?"

He said harshly, "We came out here to talk. Two men have been following us but they are well out of earshot. You know them?"

"No, but they are probably watching to make sure you do not escape." Her hand rested lightly on his arm. "You were clever to spot them, Earl. Now, shall we talk?"

They found a tavern, a small place busy with uniformed men, off-duty mercenaries returning to the economy some of the money they had been paid. The sound of their voices and laughter was a susurrating din against which no eavesdropper would stand a chance. A female dancer writhed to the music of drums and pipes, cymbals clashing on fingers, knees, wrists and ankles. An indifferent performer, but she was scantily clad and that alone was enough to please the watchers.

"Flesh," said Dephine. Her voice held disdain. "Why do men hold it in such high regard? A body, a few wisps of fabric, a little movement and they roar their pleasure. Well, that is one harlot who will do well tonight."

"You condemn her?"

"No, but the men who will pay for her dubious pleasures —surely they must know how she regards them?"

"They have fought," said Dumarest. "Some of them have killed and all have risked their lives. Every coin has two faces, my lady. And death must be matched with life."

"So the urge to destroy is accompanied by the urge to create?" She nodded, thoughtfully. "You are a philosopher, Earl. And I will admit that, even to a woman, the pressure of danger is accompanied by the desire to be loved. A risk taken, life and wealth won and then—" Her hand closed on his fingers. "The need, Earl. The overwhelming need to be taken and to share in the euphoria of love. And you, after you have fought in the arena, do you feel the same?"

"The arena?"

"You're a fighter. Don't bother to deny it. I've seen them before. Men who set their lives against their skill with a blade, who fight, hurt, kill and risk being killed for the pleasure of those who watch. And afterwards, Earl, when it's over and you walk victorious from the ring, what then?"

A table stood to one side, away from the entertainment and so unoccupied. Dumarest led the way towards it, sat, ordered wine, and looked at Dephine as a serving girl set it down.

"I have no money."

"Here." She flung coins at the girl, and as she left, said, "You haven't answered my question, Earl."

"There are more important ones. Now what is this about robbing a world?"

"An exaggeration," she admitted. "Even though the prospect is a tempting one I must admit it is impracticable. But what I propose is not. The time is ripe, the situation ideal, circumstances ensuring our success. Soldiers are everywhere and the normal police have restricted authority. In a day or so the situation will have changed which is why we must act quickly."

"We?"

She ignored the question. "A ship is on the field with clearance from the military to leave at will. A cargo is waiting and all that remains is for it to be placed aboard. Everything has been arranged and the whole thing should go without a hitch. A neat plan, Earl, there won't even be suspicion. It's simply a matter of moving goods from one place to another; from a warehouse to a ship."

"And?"

She frowned. "What do you mean, Earl? That's all there is to it. We load up and are away."

"To where?"

"Does it matter?" Her eyes were mocking. "Away from Hoghan—surely that is good enough."

A precaution and an elementary one. Kan Lofoten had to be involved but, if questioned, Dumarest couldn't implicate him. All blame must rest on the woman but, if there was trouble, she at least would have a powerful friend. And, if taken, he would be interrogated by the very man with most to hide. Dumarest could appreciate the irony of the situation even while trying to think of a way out.

"There is no way," she said, almost as if she had read his mind. "You help or you go back to your cell. You know what will happen then." Death, quickly administered to shut his mouth. "But why hesitate, Earl? The thing is foolproof."

"Then why do you need me?"

"To take care of the unknown." She was frank. "A man could be in the wrong place at the wrong time. It's a remote possibility but it exists. If so and killing has to be done then you will do it. It's your life at stake," she reminded. "Think of it."

Dumarest looked past her, at the pedestrians and soldiers moving along the street; at the men he had noticed before' who moved only to return to their original positions. Men dressed as civilians but who carried themselves with a military bearing.

"Earl?" She was impatient. "You will help?"

He said, quietly, "You realise that the penalty for looting is a particularly unpleasant form of death?"

"So?"

"One applied to both men and women without distinction?"

"That bothers you?"

"Not unless I am among those sentenced."

"You won't be," she assured. "No one will. As I told you everything has been arranged and nothing can go wrong. Earl, this is the chance of a lifetime. You will help?"

"Yes." The bottle stood between them and he poured, handing her a glass and lifting his own as if in a toast, looking past it into the green reflection of her eyes. "It seems, my lady, that I have little choice."

The room was as he had left it, the open window now framing a sleeping city. Even the noise of construction was eased except in those areas of greatest damage which, naturally, were those of greatest poverty. Dumarest thrust his head and shoulders through the opening, looked up then down, seeing nothing but sheer walls.

From where she stood in the room behind him the woman said, "Searching for enemies, Earl? Are you always so cautious?"

"It pays, my lady."

"Dephine. Call me by my name. The use of titles stultifies me." Restlessly she paced the floor; touching a vase of lambent crystal, an ornate chime from which came musical tinklings, a carved and smiling idol which nodded beneath her hand. Her feet, graced with flimsy sandals, were silent on the thick carpet. "Tell me about yourself, Earl. How did you come to be a mercenary? How often have you killed? Whom did I remind you of?"

"It would be better for you to get some sleep, my lady."

"Dephine. I can't sleep. In a few hours it will be over. Where do you come from, Earl?"

"Earth." Pausing for a moment he added, hopefully, "Have you ever heard of it?"

A hope crushed as it had been so often before by the vehemence of her reply.

"Yes, I've heard of it, and if you don't want to tell me then don't bother to lie. Earth! It's ridiculous! You might as well claim to originate on Bonanza or Avalon or El Dorado. All are worlds of legend." Annoyed, she struck at the chimes with her metallic nails. As the burst of tinkling died she snapped, "Earth! No such world exists!"

"It exists," he said. "I know. I was born on it."

"On a planet where the streams run with wine and the trees bear fruits to satisfy every need?" She made no attempt to mask her contempt. "Where no one ever grows old and there is no pain or hurt or sorrow and where everything is eternally wonderful? You were born there—and you left?"

"Earth isn't like that, Dephine. It is old and scarred with ancient wars. And yes, I left." He told her how. Stowing away as a mere boy who had more luck than he deserved. A captain who, instead of evicting him, had allowed him to work his passage and had kept him with him until he died. When, alone, the boy had moved on, ship after ship, world after world, always deeper and deeper towards the heart of the galaxy. To regions where even the very name of Earth had become a legend.

"You mean it," she said. "You really believe that you come from Earth. But, Earl, if you did you must know how to get back if that's what you want. Is it?"

"Yes."

"Then all you have to do is to find a ship going that way. You—" She broke off seeing his expression. "No?"

"No."

"But why not? Surely—"

"No one knows the coordinates," he said. "No one I have ever met knows where Earth is to be found. It lies towards the edge of the galaxy, that I know, but exactly where is something else."

"The almanacs?"

"Don't list it," he said bitterly. "You called it a world of legend and that's what most people think it is. The rest haven't even heard the name and smile when they do." He looked down at his hands, they were clenched, the knuckles white beneath the taut skin. "Smile or think they are being taken for fools."

"I'm sorry," she said quickly. "I didn't know. But what is so important about one planet? Space is full of worlds, why yearn for one?"

"I was born on it."

"And so, to you, it is home." She looked at him, her eyes gentle. "Home," she whispered. "Where else can anyone ever be happy? The fools who travel are only running from what they hope to find and, by the time they realise it, it is

too late. I hope you find your world, Earl. Your world and
your happiness and, perhaps, your woman. There is a woman?"

".No."

"Not one with red hair?" She touched her own. "You
like this color, Earl?"

"Should I?"

"Mercenaries like the color of blood. But, I forget, you
are a mercenary only by accident. Odd to think how chance
has thrown us together. Chance or fate, Earl? Were we
destined to meet before each of us even first saw the light of
day? Some would have us think so. To them everything is
foreordained and nothing we can do or attempt can alter
our destiny one iota."

"A comforting philosophy," he said.

"Comforting?" She looked at him, frowning, then smiled.
"Of course, to believe that is to absolve oneself from all
blame. A failure cannot be blamed for his failure—it is his
fate to be so. A cruel man or a weak one are not responsible for their actions. A wanton woman simply follows her
destiny. A harlot obeys the dictates of something she cannot avoid. All of us are pawns moved on a cosmic board by
some unknown player. You believe that?"

"No."

"Nor I. Life is a struggle and the rewards go to those
with the strength to take them." She moved to where the
decanter stood on a low table and poured wine into goblets. "Let us drink to that, Earl. Let us drink to success
and to happiness."

He barely touched the glass to his lips, watching as she
drank. Impatiently she set down her empty glass and stepped
towards the window. A cool breeze blew through the opening, catching her hair and sending it to stream over her
shoulders. Her profile, etched by the light, was finely chiseled
as if carved from stone.

Dumarest studied it; a face which bore the marks of
breeding as his own body bore the scars of a hard-learned
profession. One now masked with cosmetics, the hair a
flaunted challenge, the nails at variance with the hard, clean
pattern of bone, the lithe shape of the body. A woman who
for some reason had acted the harlot and could have played
the part in full. A weakness or a deliberate intent?

She said, without turning, "Why do you look at me like that?"

"I was thinking. You spoke of rewards. Just how large will my share be?"

"You are getting your life—isn't that reward enough?"

"Is it?"

"No." She turned to face him, hands lifted as if in appeal or in the opening gesture of a caress. "No! Life alone is never enough. Always there is more, for unless there is, we are no better than beasts in a field. Our senses were given us to use; our ambitions to be fulfilled. How well you understand, Earl."

"My share?"

"You will have no cause to complain, that I promise." Then, as he made no comment, she added, "I am the Lady Dephine de Monterale Keturah. My family has a reputation. Never have we broken our given word. With us it is an article of faith. I—" She broke off and shrugged. "How can I convince you? If you knew of us, Earl, you would have no doubts. And, if you want proof, then it can be given." She stepped towards him, her hands lifting to fall to his shoulders, her body coming close to press against his own. "Proof that I care for you, Earl. That I would never let you down."

Dumarest said, "It's getting late, Dephine."

"So?"

"We have other things to do."

Chapter Three

———◆———

Mist came with the dawn, a coiling, milk-white fog which blurred detail and muffled sound so that shouts turned into mumbles and shapes loomed to vanish almost at once. A state of affairs which would not last—the heat of the rising sun would quickly clear the air—but while it lasted the mist could be used.

"It's begun." Dephine glanced at a watch and slipped it into a pocket of the uniform she wore. One of black and maroon, the colors of Atlmar's Legion. Dumarest wore another. "Now remember, Earl, you do nothing unless there is need. If someone gets suspicious or acts out of line then you go in and take care of him." Her voice hardened a little. "I mean that. Don't be gentle. Kill rather than wound. There's too much at stake to be squeamish."

"And you?"

"I'll be at the ship. Luck!" Then she was gone and he was alone.

Quietly he walked along the side of the warehouse leading towards the field.

Now, for the first time, he had a chance to escape. He could hide himself deep in the city, make camp in the country, even wait until the military occupation was over. But Hoghan was a small world and in order to leave it he would have to return to the field. A convenience for anyone who could be waiting for him. A trap it was best to avoid.

He froze as a man coughed and boots crunched past in the mist. A patrolling guard or a field-worker heading for home. The noise faded and he resumed progress, one hand trailing against the wall as a guide.

The plan to rob Hoghan had been worked out by a military mind and had all the advantages of simplicity. A plan based on the fact that soldiers obeyed orders and did so without question. Instructions had been issued to load a selected cargo from a warehouse to a waiting vessel. The problem lay only in those engineering the theft being able to hide their complication—the reason for the woman, of course. She had been the 'front'.

The brain? Major Kan Lofoten. Perhaps working with someone equally ambitious. But Dumarest suspected the man to be working alone. He was too shrewd to take unnecessary chances and the plan, once decided on, would need little to put into operation.

Why include himself? As an insurance, the woman had said. A precaution. It was possible she believed that, but Dumarest wasn't so sure.

He paused as the wall fell away from beneath his fingers, turned to face right and moved a score of paces; halting as the bulk of a warehouse loomed up before him. One which should have been open by now with men busy moving crates and bales. Instead the doors remained sealed and Dumarest frowned. Something, apparently, had gone wrong.

He waited another few minutes then marched forward with a brisk step. The guard was tall, young, and startled by his sudden approach. The rifle he carried slipped from his hands and fell with a clatter.

"Who goes there? Halt and—"

"Recover your piece, soldier!"

"Yes, sir!" It swept to the salute as the man obeyed. "Colonel?"

"How long have you been with the Legion?"

"A month, sir. Just out of basic training and this is my first engagement."

"Keep better guard or it will be your last. Who is in charge here?"

"I don't know, sir."

"Who would? Lieutenant Swedel? Is he inside?" Dumarest stepped past the guard. "Keep alert, soldier. No entry for anyone without my permission. Understand?"

"Yes, sir!"

The warehouse was filled with crates, boxes, bundles, objects wreathed in sacking and rope, others cocooned in plastic. The repository of those who, knowing of the coming war, had taken steps to secure their valuables.

Swedel was a thin, stooped man with a ravaged face and

a nervous tic beneath one eye. He stared at Dumarest and, slowly, gave a salute.

"Colonel?"

"Colonel Varst. From H.Q., dispatched for Special Duties." Dumarest took papers from his pocket and fluttered them. "To be frank with you, Lieutenant, I'm in charge of Security. Undercover, you understand, but I know I can rely on your discretion. Who is in charge here?"

"Captain Risey." Swedel frowned. "Undercover Security? I don't understand."

"I think you do, Lieutenant. Where is the captain to be found?"

"He was summoned by the police an hour ago. He's probably at the garrison by now."

"The local police?" Dumarest thinned his lips as the man nodded. "Do you know why? Well, never mind, I can find out later. So that leaves you in charge. What instructions have you had for the shipping of cargo?"

"None."

"How long have you been on duty?" Dumarest saw the sudden narrowing of the eyes, the dawning suspicion. "Well, answer me, man! How long?"

"Two hours. Lieutenant Frieze collapsed from some internal complaint."

"I see." Dumarest masked his face and eyes. The unexpected had happened and the plan had failed. Swedel already suspicious, couldn't be deluded and Frieze, obviously the officer primed, was out of action. Risey? What would the police want with him?

Swedel said, "I can't understand your interest, Colonel. What has Security to do with this warehouse? And why should you think I've had instructions to ship cargo?"

"Did I say you've had?"

"No, but you inferred it. Something is wrong here." His hand dropped to his belt and the pistol holstered there. "Your identification, Colonel. I think I'd better take a closer look."

"Of course." Dumarest lifted his hand to his pocket as he looked over the other's shoulder. A group of soldiers stood before the wide doors, chatting, at ease. To one side rested a small office, the door open, a single light burning inside. "Let us go into your office."

"Your papers, Colonel!"

"In the office. You have a phone there? Good, you will be able to verify my documents—or do you trust scraps of paper more than an authorized identification?"

Dumarest headed towards it without waiting for an answer, turning as he passed through the door, the papers falling from his hand as he pulled them from his pocket. Immediately he stooped to recover them, moving as he rose to stand between the officer and the door, his bulk masking the smaller man. As Swedel reached for the useless papers Dumarest sent the stiffened fingers of his right hand stabbing at the unprotected throat. A blow designed to stun, not kill, and as the man slumped Dumarest caught him, supporting him in his arms.

"Sir?" One of the soldiers, attracted by the hint of movement, was looking towards the office. "Is anything wrong?"

"Nothing." Dumarest turned towards him, one arm behind Swedel's back, his hand gripping the belt to hold the man upright. "Get those doors open! You have a loading platform? Good. Have it prepared. Move!"

As they sprang to obey, Dumarest eased his limp burden into the only chair the office contained, turned it to face the phone, propping the head on the folded arms. To a casual glance he was a man engrossed in making a call.

"Sir?" A soldier called to Dumarest as he left the office. "What shall we load?"

The platform was pulled by a mechanical horse, a small, whining vehicle which dragged it across the field through veils of mist. It held a dozen crates, boxes chosen from a pile standing beside the doors and which Dumarest could only hope held things of value. There had been no time to make sure.

The soldiers who had loaded them walked at the rear of the platform. The driver, squinting ahead, cursed the mist as he strained to see his destination.

"The *Varden*, sir?"

"To the east of the field." The mist was both a help and a hindrance—and why hadn't Dephine placed the guide beacon? Dumarest pushed ahead, almost running, seeing it after he had covered a hundred yards, a winking, yellow glow. Dephine stood beneath it.

"Earl?"

"Is everything arranged?"

"Yes. Where is the loot?"

"Coming—what I could get of it." Dumarest turned as the thin whine of the vehicle grew louder. "Something went wrong. Get inside and out of that uniform. Have the captain ready to leave when I give the word. Hurry!"

"He won't be rushed, Earl. It wasn't supposed to be like this. He—"

"Will do as I tell him!" Dumarest snarled his impatience. "Don't stand there arguing, woman. We're racing against time. Now get in the ship and have the handler standing by. The loading ramp should be moving and the ports open. I—" He broke off as a dull report echoed through the air. "Guns."

"A diversion," she explained. "I arranged it. It should distract the guards."

Men bribed to fire into the air at a certain time, but they were late, a thing she hadn't yet realised.

"Earl?"

"The plan failed," he said, quickly. "The officer who was supposed to have taken care of the loading fell ill and his replacement knew nothing about it. The police are involved somehow and they could be moving in. Now get busy. If this ship leaves without us we're as good as dead. If it doesn't leave at all, the same. You take care of the captain while I see the handler. Are you armed?" He grunted as she showed him a compact laser. "Don't use it unless you have to, but don't hesitate to burn a hole if you must."

He ran into the ship as she vanished through the port. The handler, a sallow-faced man, straightened from where he leaned against a bulkhead. He scowled as Dumarest snapped orders.

"Now wait a minute, mister. I'm not one of your soldier-boys to jump when you give the word. You've got a cargo to be loaded? Right, we'll load it, but all in good time."

"My time," said Dumarest. "Get that ramp started and get to work. Never mind stacking the stuff, just get it aboard."

"Now wait a minute!" The handler gulped as Dumarest reached out towards him, gripped him, sank his fingers into yielding flesh. "You—I can't breathe!"

"You can breathe," said Dumarest. "But not for long if you keep arguing. Now get to it and let me see you move."

The platform was approaching when he ducked through the port, coming to a halt as Dumarest reached the ground.

The handler, scared, had started the belt and Dumarest snapped at the man to throw the crates on the moving surface. As the first vanished into the ship a soldier tensed, head turned, listening as the sound of gunfire came closer.

"Something's up, Colonel. An attack of some kind."

"Just noise. Keep working." Dumarest looked at the beacon. It would attract unwanted attention and it had served its purpose. He mounted the ramp, lifted it from its support and switched off the pulsing, yellow glow. As it died a bullet smashed the instrument from his hands.

"You at the ship!" The voice, amplified, roared from the mist. "You haven't a chance. Surrender!"

"Sir?" The soldiers, bemused, stared up at where Dumarest stood. "What's happening, Colonel?"

"Nothing."

"We're being fired on!" A soldier grabbed his rifle from the platform, freezing as the voice thundered around them.

"This is Colonel Emridge speaking. I order all soldiers of the Legion to refuse to obey all orders from any officer but myself. If they are with an officer they must place him under arrest. This is a direct command from the highest level. If any officer attempts to escape he is to be shot down."

"I guess that means you, Colonel." The soldier with the rifle lifted it to his shoulder. "Move and I'll let you have it."

The port was open behind him, the door swung back, a slab of solid metal more than proof against a bullet. But the man had his finger on the trigger, the weapon aimed and ready to fire.

Dumarest called, loudly, "No! Don't kill him! Don't shoot!"

He saw the barrel of the rifle drop as the man instinctively turned and was diving into the ship before he could realise how he'd been tricked. A bullet slammed against the hull, another against the door as he dogged it tight.

"Dephine?" Dumarest slapped his hand against the communicator as he called. "Dephine?"

"Here, Earl." Her voice was small over the speaker, strained, but that was to be expected. "In the control room."

"Coming. Have the captain order total seal."

Dumarest released the button and made his way through the ship, passing closed doors and familiar compartments. In the empty salon he paused, slipping the knife from his boot and tucking it into the belt of his uniform. As he reached the control room he called, "Dephine?"

"Here, Earl. Inside."

She stood beside the control chair, out of uniform now, her clothing crumpled, her hair a mess. Her hands, empty, were extended towards him.

Dumarest turned, snatching at his knife, freezing as he saw the man behind him, the knuckle white on the trigger of the laser pointed at his stomach.

Major Kan Lofoten smiled.

He stood very tall and very confident against the edge of the door, neat in his uniform, the gun no less menacing than his eyes.

He said, "As I promised, Captain. You see how an intelligent brain can determine the course of events? Either way we win."

Dumarest looked at the woman.

"He was waiting, Earl. Here in the control room. He disarmed me before I had a chance." Swallowing she added, "When I came to talk to the captain he—"

"Shall we say that I took over?" Lofoten gestured with the gun. "But then I have been in charge all along. Even your clever scheme, my dear, which was not so clever when duly considered, was more the result of my hints than your own intelligence. To steal from a mercenary band. How little you know of how the military operate. And yet there was a chance the thing could succeed given the right kind of fool."

Dumarest said, "We have some loot so why the gun? Why not just let us go? That was the original intention, wasn't it? To let us go and to take full blame for your previous thefts. What happened, Major? Did someone find out what you'd done?"

"Be silent!"

"Why?" Dumarest glanced at the captain who stood, a thick-set, swarthy man before the glittering tell-tales of the main console. "Captain Remille might be interested. To me it was obvious—why else should you trust a stranger? For what other reason than to act as a catspaw and decoy? But you had me fooled for a while when I learned that Lieutenant Frieze had fallen sick. I took him to be your man. I was wrong."

"Sick?" Remille frowned. "Another one?"

"Shut up, you fool!"

"Yes, Captain, shut up," said Dumarest cynically. "You're on your own vessel and in full command but you must remain silent when the officer speaks. After all he is a member of a mercenary band. A disgraced member, true, and one who will be shot when they get their hands on him, but you must remain silent until he gives you permission to speak."

"Talk again and I'll fire!" snapped Lofoten. "Don't listen to him, Remille."

"Why not, Captain? He talks sense." Dephine edged closer. "What does Lofoten bring you? Nothing. We have a dozen crates filled with valuables. More than enough to buy passage. What further use can the Major be to you?"

"You bitch! I'll—"

Lofoten lifted the gun, raising it high to bring it slashing across her face, a vicious blow which would have opened her cheek, smashed her nose, torn her lips and turned the clean lines of her face into a puffed ugliness.

Dumarest caught his wrist before the gun could fall. His fingers tightened, twisting, his body moving as the laser fell from the nerveless fingers, the trapped arm slamming across his chest, the sound of snapping bone like the breaking of a twig.

"The gun!" He caught it as she threw it towards him. "Get your own." The knife made a soft slithering as he tucked it back into his boot. "Cover them while I get off this uniform." He kicked aside the discarded fabric. "Well, Captain?"

"We had a deal," said Remille glancing towards Lofoten. "Crates slipped aboard and goods to be sold on a secret market. That's all I know but I had to deal through the woman. Then he arrived on board and—well, the rest you know."

"And the sick men?"

Remille avoided his eyes. "Nothing."

He was lying, but Dumarest couldn't guess why and had no time to find out. Already the mercenaries would be assembling heavy equipment to break into the ship and metal, protection against a bullet, was of little defence against a heavy missile.

From where he sat on the deck, Lofoten said, "Captain, if I could talk with you in private?" He heaved himself to his feet, his arm hanging limply at his side. His face was pale, beaded with sweat. "It's important."

Dumarest said, "Captain, are you ready to leave?"

"Yes, but—"

"Wait much longer and you won't get the chance. Those outside will split your hull open like a rotten melon. My guess is they have charges set and ready to go." Dumarest gestured towards the panel where a signal lamp flashed in ruby urgency. "The radio-attention signal. They want to talk to you."

"Let them want. Damned mercenaries, strutting and swaggering. To hell with them."

"Is your crew aboard?"

"All but the steward. He—we can do without a steward." Remille made up his mind. "We leave." Then, looking at Lofoten, he said, "What about him?"

"Kick him out."

"Let me come with you! Captain! Please!"

"Dump him," snapped Dumarest. "Drop him through the lower hatch. It's him they want, not us."

"Earl, they'll kill him." Dephine's voice was high. "You know the kind of death they give to looters."

He said, bitterly, "He would have smashed in your face had I let him. He would have burned me down given the chance. To hell with him." Reaching out he grabbed the man's good arm. "Let's get rid of this filth and be on our way."

Chapter Four

The *Varden* was small; a roving free-trader picking up a living wherever a cargo was to be found; the crew paid if and when there were profits to be shared. Aside from the looted crates the hold was empty; but there were passengers.

Dumarest studied them a day later as he sat in the salon. At the table a fat man toyed with a deck of cards, ringed hands deft as he manipulated the pasteboards. Charl Tao, a dealer in rare and precious merchandise—or so he claimed. Dumarest had a shrewd suspicion that the salves and lotions which formed his stock in trade contained not the near-magical essences he said but ingredients of a more humble origin.

Glaring at the plump trader a thin-faced, wasp-voiced woman sat in the rigid attitude of one who wore unyielding garments. Allia Mertrony, a widow, a follower of some obscure sect. Her cabin stank of incense and she wore a cap of dark material covering her hair. Next to her sat a middle-aged man with a bandaged leg. Fren Harmond, taciturn, his face creased with pain.

"A game, Earl?" Charl glanced towards Dumarest. "Something to pass the time. Spectrim, starsmash, banko, man-in-between. You name it and we'll play it."

"For money, no doubt," snapped the woman.

"For small stakes and those only to add interest. How about you, Fren, it'll take your mind off the pain."

"No."

"You don't have to suffer it," said Charl smoothly. "I've a few drops which will give you dreams instead of anguish. Come to my cabin and let's see what can be done."

"We should have a steward," said the woman. "It's all very well to say that he was too sick to rejoin us on Hoghan but we should have one just the same. It's a part of the service."

Dumarest said, "Did any of you board at Hoghan?"

"We came from Legand," said the plump man. "I wanted to leave but they wouldn't let me and when I learned why I was pleased to change my mind."

"They wouldn't let you land? Why not?"

"The war. Surely you must have been involved. We arrived at a bad time and it was best to remain within the safety of the ship. So Captain Remille advised and he made sense."

"Did you book to Hoghan?"

"No, to Malach. The ship had a special delivery to make. It adds time to the journey, but what choice had we?"

"We should have a steward," said the old woman fretfully. "Who is to give us quick-time? Or are we supposed to do without? I've paid for a High Passage and I want what I've paid for. Fren, why don't you complain to the captain? Charl—"

"I'll do it," said Dumarest.

In the control room the air was alive with the hums and burrs of smoothly working apparatus, the sensors questing their way into space, plotting a path and guiding the vessel with mechanical efficiency. Remille sat in his chair, the navigator at his post beside him. A thin man with sour lips half-hidden beneath a ruff of beard, Haw Mayna had an abrupt and bristling manner.

"What do you want? Passengers aren't allowed in the control room. Damn it, man, surely you must know that!"

"Captain?"

"He's right." Remille turned to glare from the depths of his chair. "What is it?"

"You haven't a steward," said Dumarest. "I'm applying for the job." He sensed the hesitation, caught the glance each threw to the other. "I've done it before. Worked as a handler too. I know what has to be done."

"Let him do it," said the navigator after a moment. "Anything for peace. Just keep them quiet and happy."

The previous steward had been allocated a cabin at the end of the passage. It was bare, not even the cabinet containing a scrap of clothing. The bunk was stripped of bedding. The set of drawers normally filled with small items of personal value, like the cabinet, were empty.

Thoughtfully Dumarest moved back to the small room

adjoining the salon. From a drawer he took a hypogun and loaded it with quick-time. Charl smiled at him as he moved towards the man.

"Throat or wrist?"

"Throat. It's more efficient."

"If you aim straight, I agree." The man tilted his head, exposing the side of his neck. "Go ahead."

Dumarest aimed the instrument, touched the trigger and it was done. Carried by a blast of air the drug penetrated the skin and fat to mingle directly in the bloodstream. The effect was immediate. As if stricken, Charl Tao slowed, turned into an apparent statue, not even his eyes moving as Dumarest moved to the others and treated each in turn. At the door of the salon he turned to look at them. All three were apparently frozen, their metabolism slowed by the chemical magic of quick-time so that, to them, normal hours passed as swiftly as minutes, weeks shrank into days. A convenience to relieve the tedium of long voyages.

Dephine was in her cabin. She had been sleeping but, as Dumarest entered, she woke to sit upright, stretching her arms above her head. Rest had taken some of the tiny lines of strain from around her eyes, but anticipation made her features even more sharp.

"Now, Earl?"

"Not yet."

"How long must we wait? Those crates are just begging to be examined. Who knows what we may have won? A fortune! Enough to keep us in luxury for the rest of our lives!" She saw the hypogun in his hand. "What's this?" She smiled when he told her. "So you're the new steward. A clever move, Earl. A crew member has advantages the passengers lack. Now hurry! Treat the others and let's see what we have!"

The crates lay in an untidy heap to one side of the hold, held only by a single lashing of rope, the restraint less than useless had the ship been subjected to sudden strain. Dumarest slashed it free and hauled at the topmost box. It thudded to the deck, the lid starting from its seating. With a jerk he tore it free. Beneath lay a mass of fibre which Dephine tore apart with her bare hands.

"Earl? What the hell—"

The crate was stacked with guns. Antiques. Each individually wrapped in plastic, each weapon carefully labeled. Dumarest lifted one, a rifle with a chased stock and an elaborate sight. The barrel was flared and the trigger of a peculiar shape.

"A hunting rifle made for the Mangate of Tyrone after the accident which deformed the muscles of his right hand. He—"

"Never mind that!" Dephine snatched the weapon from his hands as Dumarest read the label. "What about the others?"

They were all much the same, items which belonged to a collection or a museum, and with the thought came the answer.

"We took the wrong boxes." Dumarest turned one, read the small label previously unnoticed. "This comes from the Hargromond Collection. They packed the guns and put them into the warehouse for safe-keeping." He frowned at her expression. "I had no time to choose," he reminded. "These boxes were stacked close to the door and I figured they were the ones due for shipment. Blame Lofoten, not me."

"I don't blame you, Earl," she said quickly. "You did your best. No one could have done better. Let's look at the others."

Two held scraps of pottery and fragments of ceramic, another mouldering reports and carefully bound books which Dumarest checked then put aside. Had they been early navigational tables they would have held interest; as it was they were ancient histories of the first settlers, valuable only to those concerned.

Dephine drew in her breath as she dug into another crate. "Earl!"

Beneath a layer of faded clothing rested small packets of opaque material. One, opened, rested in her hands, the sparkle of gems reflected in her eyes. A cache of jewels, carefully hidden, placed among items of small value for added concealment.

"Check the others." Dumarest watched as more gems came into view: a tiara, necklaces, pendant earrings, bracelets. All were of delicate workmanship, all old, all of high value. As Dephine slipped rings on her fingers, extending her hands to admire them, he said, "See what else that box contains."

"What do you think they are worth, Earl?"

"Our lives." He was grim. "If the others spot what we have how long do you think they would let us keep it?"

"The captain?"

"He and the others of the crew. They are little better than pirates." Replacing the lids they had removed Dumarest shifted the checked boxes to reach others lower down. "Hide those gems, Dephine. Find a place in your cabin for now and I'll look for a better one later on."

"We'll have to leave something, Earl. Remille would never believe that we had escaped with a load of rubbish."

A good point and one he had thought of, but the other crates might provide the answer. Items of value but too bulky to be easily hidden. Things it would take a specialist to sell, such as the antique guns, the mouldering books, the plaques of intricate workmanship valuable more for their designs than for the basic material.

They could be shown to the captain and shared with him. The portable loot he would keep.

Stooping he moved a crate to one side, cleared the lid of the one below, set his fingers at the edge and heaved. It resisted his tug and he leaned forward to study it. It seemed more sturdy than the others they had checked, thick wood fastened with heavy screws. The end held a red daub the others lacked. Others, similarly marked, rested at the bottom of the heap.

"Earl?"

"These are different," he said. "The soldiers must have mixed the consignment or just took those nearest to hand. I had no time to check."

"We'll need tools to open this." Dephine tugged at the lid. "Something of real value must rest inside and there are more than one. Earl! This could be it!"

The fortune everyone yearned for, hoped to obtain, dreamed of during the long, lonely hours. The magic which would turn a hell into a paradise—or so they thought. Too often sudden wealth ruined what was barely flawed, accentuated traits which would have been innocuous if left unstimulated.

He said, patiently. "Dephine, we have money. The gems."

"There could be more!" She tore at the lid, her nails scratching the wood, making ugly, tearing sounds. "Get some tools, Earl! Hurry!"

He fetched them from the engine room where the engineer sat facing the handler, a chess board between them, the bent fingers of the officer hovering over a pawn. It was a fraction of an inch away when Dumarest entered to select the tools. It had barely touched by the time he left. The move itself could take minutes of normal time.

Back in the hold Dumarest set to work. The screws yielded as he strained on the tool, lifting to be thrown aside. A dozen screws, a score, and the lid was free to be lifted. It made a dull thud as it hit the deck.

"Earl!" Dephine's voice held incredulous amazement. "Earl, what—"

The crate held a corpse.

The body was that of a girl, young, once attractive, but now ugly with the blotches which marked her face and shoulders, the arms crossed on the chest, her hands. Small blotches of an ebon darkness, rimmed with scarlet, looking like velvet patches stuck on with a ruby glue, each the size of the tip of a finger.

Dephine said, shakily, "She's dead, Earl. Dead. But why put her into a box?"

Not a box, a coffin, her presence had turned a container into something special, but Dumarest didn't correct the woman. He leaned close, studying the lines of the dead face, the hollows of the cheeks and shoulders. The body was wrapped in plain white fabric from beneath the armpits to a little above the knees. The feet, long and slim, were bare, blotched as were the shins, the thighs.

"Earl?"

Dumarest moved, seeing the play of refracted light on the hair, silver strands which shimmered beneath the plastic envelope into which the body had been placed.

"For God's sake, Earl! Answer me! What's all this about?"

Dumarest said, slowly, "I'm not sure. Let's open another crate. One with the same markings."

Like the other it contained death, this time an elderly man, his face seamed, the brows tufted, the knuckles of his blunt-fingered hands scarred. Like the girl his body was marked with blotches. Like her he had been sealed in a plastic bag.

"Another." Dephine stared at the rest of the marked crates. "They're all coffins. I don't understand. Why stack

them in a warehouse?" Her voice rose to hover on the edge
of hysteria. "Earl, we've stolen a load of dead meat. A
bunch of corpses. How the hell are they going to make us
rich?"

"Stop it!" His hand landed on her cheek, red welts mark-
ing the impact of his fingers. "You aren't a child. You've
seen dead men before, women too, so why be stupid?"

"You're right." She rubbed at her cheek. "It was just that
I didn't expect to see corpses in those crates. They must
have been packed away for later cremation or burial. But
why do that?"

"The war."

"People die in war."

"Dephine—it depends what they died of."

"Earl?" She frowned, not understanding then said sharply,
as he attacked the rest of the boxes, "No! If they contain
more dead I don't want to see them. Leave it, Earl. Let
the captain open them if he wants to."

Dumarest ignored the suggestion. The first two contained
the bodies of a man and a woman, both middle-aged. The
third held the shape of a slender man with a roached and
dyed beard. The backs of his arms were heavily tattooed.
Among the lurid designs was a name.

"The *Varden*." Dumarest sat back on his heels. "This must
be the missing steward."

"Dead and sealed in a crate?" said Dephine blankly, then,
as she realised the implication, added, "No, Earl! My God,
not that!"

It couldn't be anything else. Dumarest remembered the
stacked crates, the soldiers on duty, the Lieutenant's suspi-
cions. And the gunfire he had thought a distraction which
had come too late.

"Plague," he said. "It was in the city. Maybe the steward
carried it or maybe he picked it up, either way he fell sick
and died. The dead needed to be disposed of but with the
city at war that wasn't too easy. A soldier could have seen
something, put two and two together, and there would
have been a riot. As it was the news must have leaked out."

"How can you say that?"

"I forget, you couldn't know. The officer at the warehouse, Lieutenant Frieze, fell sick and had to be taken from
his post. I thought he was Lofoten's man, then I didn't, but
he must have had the disease. The police summoned his su-

perior to a conference. Maybe they wanted soldiers to ring the field. If the populace grew panic-stricken they would have rushed for transport away from Hoghan. The gunfire we heard was to beat them back, men firing into the air—it doesn't matter."

"Lofoten—the bastard!"

"I don't think he knew until the end."

"He wanted to come with us, Earl. To escape."

Perhaps, but he could have had another reason. And no sane man would willingly have placed himself in the position they were now in. It took a few moments for the woman to realise it.

"Earl! If the steward contracted the disease?"

"He died of it."

"But where? Here in the ship? Even if he didn't actually die in the vessel he could have brought it into the *Varden* with him. He slept here. And Remille. He didn't want to stay. He wouldn't even answer the radio-summons. He must have guessed that the authorities on Hoghan intended to seize the ship and place it in quarantine. And we thought they were worried about a little loot. A mess." She looked at her hands, they were trembling, little shimmers darting from her nails. "And you, Earl. You were in the warehouse where that officer fell sick. You could have touched what he did. Even now—"

"Yes," said Dumarest. "It's possible."

"My God, Earl! What should we do?"

"Get the captain. Let him see what we've found then dump the crates into space."

"And?"

"Wait," he said grimly. "And, if you've a mind to, pray."

Chapter Five

Allia Mertrony did the praying, kneeling before a disc of polished brass, the bright orb wreathed in plumes of fuming incense. Her voice was a high, keening ululating chant, echoing from the bulkheads, scratching at the nerves.

"Listen to her!" Charl Tao scowled as he faced Dumarest in the corridor. "Can't you put a stop to it, Earl? Praying's one thing but this howling is getting me down."

"It's her way."

"Maybe, but it isn't mine." Charl rubbed the backs of his hands, a common gesture now, as was the quick glance he gave them. "A pity she had to know."

Dumarest said, flatly, "She had the right."

"And she would have found out anyway." Charl shook his head as the sound rose to grate at the ears. "Who would have thought an old crone like that had such powerful lungs? It comes with practice, I suppose. Earl?"

"Nothing."

"As yet." Charl rubbed his hands again, halting the gesture with an obvious effort. "To hell with it. If it gets me, it gets me. Come to my cabin later, I've a special bottle we might as well share while we can enjoy it."

"Later," said Dumarest.

He walked through the ship, stood in the hold, totally empty now aside from the caskets used to transport beasts and which, more often than not, held men. Those traveling Low, doped, frozen and ninety per cent dead, risking the fifteen per cent death rate for the sake of cheap travel. He had ridden that way too often, watching the lid close firmly over his face, sinking into oblivion and thinking as blackness closed around him, "this time . . . ?"

A gamble he had won so far, but no luck could last forever.

Aside from the lack of crates nothing seemed to have changed. The same, blue-white light streamed down from the bulbs and threw the stained paint and shabby furnishings into sharp relief.

As familiar a scene as were the cabins, the salon, the corridors and appointments of the ship. As was the faint vibration of the Erhaft field which sent the vessel hurtling through space. He had traveled on a hundred such ships and worked on many of them. They were a form of home, a pattern into which he could fit. But the *Varden* was different now. Something had been added. Something small, invisible, unknown.

The threat of the final illness.

Each had met it in their own way.

To Allia Mertrony it was a time for prayer. God was good and would help, but first God had to be aroused and informed of her need. Lars would see to that. Ten years dead now he would be waiting. Drifting in a state akin to sleep, until she should join him, so that together they could continue their journey into the infinite. A mating for life and eternity, so her sect was convinced, and two-thirds of her life had been spent making certain she had found the right man. The cap she wore to hide the temptation of her hair was a public announcement that she was sworn to another.

The bulkheads quivered to the force of her wordless ululations.

The disc before which she knelt was not an idol but a focus for her thoughts. The incense was a sacrifice blessed by tradition. Her prayers were to inform Lars of her condition, to prepare him for her coming if that was to be. To wake him to intercede on her behalf. Not to be saved, for death was inevitable, and to live beyond the allotted span a sin, but to die bravely. So let there be no pain. Let her face and figure escape further ravishment, not for the sake of pride but for the dignity a man expected in his mate.

Soon now, soon—if God willed, they would be together.

In the engine room the handler and the engineer sat at their board playing endless games of chess, snarling at any who came too close. Firm in a limited area of isolation, they ate food from cans and drank from bottles sealed with heavy gobs of wax. Nurtured stores bought with past gains; small luxuries which normally would have been doled out a little at a time, now used with wanton extravagance for a double reason. Sealed they would be uncontaminated, used they would not be wasted.

Dephine remained in her cabin, taking endless mist-showers, anointing her body with salves Charl provided, adorning herself with the gems they had found.

She turned as Dumarest entered the cabin, tall, sparkling with jewels and precious metal. Her hair, dressed, provided a cradle for the tiara. The earrings fell from her ears to almost touch her shoulders. At throat and wrists reflected light shone with the lurid glow of trapped fires, green and red, amber and azure, the clear blue of sapphires, the splintered glow of diamonds.

Slamming the door he said, "You fool!"

"Why? Because I like what we found?" She turned before him, her dress stained, the jewels making her appear tawdry and, somehow, cheap.

"What if someone else had come into the cabin?"

"They wouldn't. I had it locked."

"You didn't."

"Then I forgot. But who would dare to walk in like you did? No one owns me, Earl. Not even you."

He said, cruelly, "The Lady Dephine de Monterale Keturah. A woman who comes from a family which values pride above all. Isn't that what you told me?"

"So?"

"They should see you now. Not even the cheapest harlot would dress herself like that."

"You bastard!"

He caught her hands as they rose towards his face, halting the nails as they stabbed towards his eyes, his fingers hard around her wrists, tight against the bone. She strained, spat into his face, jerked up a knee in a vicious blow to the groin. He twisted, taking it on the thigh, then pushed her back and away to slam hard against the far wall.

"Do that again and you'll regret it," he said coldly.

"You'd do what—slice off my fingers?" Her sneer turned to trepidation as she looked at his face, saw the cold eyes, the mouth grown suddenly cruel. "You'd do it," she said. "You'd really do it."

He said nothing, wiping the spittle off his cheek.

"Earl!" Afraid now, she was contrite. "I—you shouldn't have said what you did. You had no right."

"Look at yourself, woman!" Catching her shoulder he turned her to face the full-length mirror. "Dressed in gems looted from the dead. Have you no sense?"

"They didn't come from the dead! Earl, you know that! They were in a separate cache. I—" She broke off, a hand lifting to touch the tiara. "You don't think that girl wore this before she died? Some cultures destroy personal possessions with the dead. Earl?"

"No." To frighten her further would serve no purpose and the damage, if damage there was, had been done. "Get rid of those things. Hide them."

Slowly she removed the gems, letting them fall into a glittering heap on the bunk.

"Fren Harmond was talking, Earl. He can't understand why Remille doesn't return to Hoghan. They could have a vaccine there by now. He wanted Charl to join him in a deputation."

"He's wasting his time."

"Maybe, but Remille's only human and what good is a ship to a dead man? He might decide to take a chance on the penalties. If he does we're in trouble, Earl. Kan Lofoten would have spilled his guts about what we did. If they ever got us they would kill us. Atlmar's Legion isn't noted for being gentle." Pausing she added, "They could even follow us. Have you thought of that?"

"Yes."

"And?"

"You don't tell a captain to change course unless you have good reason," said Dumarest. "I've tried and he isn't interested. He needs more than words."

Fren Harmond provided it. He sat in his cabin, his bandaged leg supported before him, his face seamed and graven with lines of pain. A stubborn man, refusing the drugs Dumarest had offered which would have eased his anguish. A fanatic who believed that the body would heal itself if left alone.

"It's killing me!" The leg twitched as he moved it, beads of sweat dewing his forehead. "The pain—Earl, help me!"

Charl Tao stood at the other side of the sick man. Meeting Dumarest's eyes he shrugged.

"My friend, I have done my best, but what use is skill

when dealing with a fool? I've offered him the surcease of dreams. I have a salve which will knit bone and abolish scars, add muscle and strengthen tissue if used in the correct manner. I—"

"You're not in a market now, Charl. Be serious." Dumarest touched the flesh above the bandages. It was febrile, the skin scabrous to the touch. "How did you do this?"

"I was out climbing. I slipped and hurt the ankle. Yield to a small pain and it will get worse so I made my way back home. The ship was due and I had to get to the field. A local man applied the bandage."

"A doctor?"

"A tradesman—he had the cloth."

"And it hurt then as it does now?"

"It hurt, but not as badly. Pain is the signal that the flesh is healing itself and to be expected in case of injury. But it is getting worse, more than I can bear."

Which should mean, following the man's own logic, that the injury was almost well. An anomaly which Dumarest didn't mention as he removed the bandages.

Charl Tao sucked in his breath at the sight of the wound.

"Harmond, my friend, you have a problem."

A bad one. The flesh around and above the ankle was puffed and streaked with ugly strands of red, parts of it so purple as to be almost black. A broken place oozed a thick, yellow pus and the wound held a sickly stench. The result of infection, gangrene, poisons, carried into the broken skin from stale clothing. The cause no longer mattered.

"Earl?"

"It's bad. Does this hurt? And this?" Dumarest pressed his fingers along the length of the leg. "Have you a swelling in the groin? Yes?" His fingers touched the spot through the clothing, meeting a hard node of swollen tissue in the crease between the leg and stomach. One of the major lymph glands acting as a defence against the poisons. "That will have to be lanced to ease the pressure. A drain fitted. The ankle needs to be cauterized—you've dead tissue there which must be burned away."

"No!" Harmond shook his head. "Not the use of drugs and fire. Not the touch of iron. The body will heal itself given the chance."

"You asked me to help you."

"Yes, to change the dressing, to ease the pain in some

way. Some have that power. By the touch of their hands they can bring peace.

"Earl is one of them," said Charl dryly. "But the peace he gives is permanent. He does it like this." His hands reached for the sick man's throat; thick fingers pressed sharply and lifted as the head lolled. "Quickly, Earl! Give him the drugs before he recovers!"

Dumarest lifted the hypogun and blasted sleep-inducing drugs into the unconscious man's throat. Changing the setting and load of the instrument he fired it around the wounded ankle, heavy doses of antibiotics coupled with compounds to block the nerves and end the transmission of pain.

"Help me get him on his bunk," he ordered. "Strip and wash him and then you can operate."

"Me?"

"You have the skill," said Dumarest. "And the knowledge. The way you put him out—a trick taught to the monks of the Church of Universal Brotherhood. A pressure on sensitive nerves, as good as an anesthetic if applied with skill. You've had medical training, Charl. You deny it?"

The plump man shrugged. "A few years in a medical school, Earl, in which I gained a few elementary facts and some basic knowledge. Then something happened—a woman, but there is no need to go into detail. Just let me say that it became imperative to travel." He looked at his hands. "But I have never operated since that time."

"Then it's time you began. Tell me what you need and I'll see if it's in the ship. If it isn't you'll have to make out the best you can."

"You'll help me?"

"No, I'm going to see the captain."

Crouched like a spider in its lair, Captain Remille sat in his great chair and dreamed. Around him the web of electronic impulses searched space and hung like a protective curtain about his ship. From an outside viewpoint the shimmering field of the drive would have turned the scarred vessel into a comet-like thing of beauty but inside where he sat only the glow of tell-tales, the brilliant glory of the screens, relieved the gloom.

A buzz and he tensed, a click and he relaxed. The warning had been taken care of. The ship had made a minute correction in its headlong flight and a scrap of interstellar matter, perhaps no larger than a pea, had been safely avoided.

Sinking back, he looked at the screens.

Always he enjoyed the spectacle of naked space, the blaze of scattered stars, the sheets and curtains of glowing luminescence, the haloed blotches of dust clouds, the fuzz of distant nebulae. Stars uncountable, worlds without end, distances impossible to contemplate with the limited abilities of the mind.

Remille didn't try it. More than one captain had been driven insane by contemplation of the cosmos, fantasies born in distorted minds, the product of wild radiations and wilder rumors. Things lived in space, or so it was hinted, great beings with gossamer wings which caught the light of suns and carried them like drifting smears of moonlight across the voids. And other creatures which no one living had ever seen. Ravenous beasts which lurked in space as great fish lurked in seas, waiting to rend ships and men.

The proof had been found in wreckage ripped plates bearing unnatural scars, crews which had vanished without apparent cause, empty hulks which had been gutted and robbed of life. If living entities hadn't done such things then what had?

Questions asked by old men in taverns, echoed by romantic fools. Space, to Remille, was something to be crossed. Dangers to avoid. All he had in life was the ship—he could do without imagination.

"Captain?"

"What is it?" Remille turned to stare at Dumarest. "Trouble?"

"A man is sick." The truth even though Remille must think it other than what it was. "Fren Harmond."

"The one with the bad leg?"

"Yes."

"A fool, one almost as bad as the old woman with her noise." Remille made an impatient gesture. "Well, you know what to do. Complete isolation."

None to get too near to another, a thing he and the navigator had followed from the first hint that disease could be aboard. Haw Mayna was in his cabin now, probably locked in a drugged sleep, there was little for him to do once the course was set.

"I've attended to it," said Dumarest. "Captain, are you still heading for Malach?"

"That's our destination."

"They could be waiting. Word could have been sent ahead, but you must have thought of that. Do you think they will permit us to land?"

Remille bared his teeth, yellow bone which looked as if covered with oil in the light from the screens.

"I'll land. How the hell can they stop me?"

"And?"

A thing Remille had thought of, a problem for which he had found no answer. A suspected ship was unwanted on any planet and Malach was not a gentle world. If he carried disease and tried to land the ship would be confiscated, himself and the others placed in six-month quarantine, heavy fines and penalties ordered against him. At the end he would be worse than ruined.

"You carry no cargo," said Dumarest. "No one will have reason to complain if you don't reach Malach."

"The passengers?"

"I'll take care of them. They can be compensated and found passage on another ship." Dumarest added, quickly, "That can be arranged, surely?"

"Passages cost money."

"And so does delay. They won't want to be quarantined with all the cost that entails. Charl Tao will agree and the woman can be persuaded."

"And Harmond?"

"As I told you, Captain, he's sick." Dumarest paused, waiting, then relaxed as Remille, coming to a decision, nodded. "Tell the navigator to report to me at once."

Mayna didn't respond to the knock at his door. Dumarest knocked again then tested the lock. The door opened as he pressed to reveal the man sitting cross-legged on his bunk. His eyes were rimmed with pus, veined with red, the pupils contracted to pin-points. Before him, lying on the cover, was a paper covered with a lewd design.

Dumarest folded it, held his hand before the staring eyes, moved it from side to side. The pupils remained stationary, looking at the point where the paper had lain. In imagination the navigator was a living participant in what the design had portrayed. Until the drug he had absorbed had been neutralised or had run its course he would remain deaf and blind to external stimulae.

From the door Charl said, "Earl, there is something you should see."

"It must wait. The captain wants Mayna to report to him immediately. Did you provide him with his amusement?"

"A simple thing, Earl, and harmless. Life can be hard and lonely for those who live in space and who can begrudge them a dream? You care to try one? I have patterns and compounds to induce illusions of love, of adventure, of unbridled luxury and domestic bliss. Oddly the latter is the one in greatest demand. A loving and faithful wife, children, the sweetness of contained passion. Or—"

"Get him out of it."

"Earl, I can't! The dream must run its course." Charl leaned forward and touched the man's temple, the great arteries in the throat. "It won't be long now. The acceleration of the heart, the growing warmth of the skin—soon it will be over and he will wake. But this I can do." His plump hands moved with sure dexterity as he scrawled a message with a crayon on the back of the pattern. "There, when he wakes he will see it and obey. Now, Earl, please come with me."

"Harmond?"

He lay supine on his bunk, his face relaxed, his body naked from the waist down. Bandages covered his ankle and the air held the taint of charred flesh. A drain had been set in the lanced swelling of his groin; a thin, plastic tube held with sticky tape to permit the escape of accumulated fluids. The thing had a professional look about it as did the bandage.

"Did you have to burn deep?"

"Almost to the bone but I think we caught it in time. But that's not what I wanted to show you." Charl lifted the edge of the shirt and drew it upwards over the stomach and the lower ribs. "There, Earl. There!"

Dumarest followed the guide of the pointing finger, seeing a small, ebon blotch, a patch of velvety darkness rimmed with a thin band of angry red.

Chapter Six

———————

Throwing back her hair Dephine said, "So Fren's got it. Well, I guess we can't all be lucky. How bad is it, Earl?"

"It's too early to tell."

"And you were close to him. Earl—you fool!"

"Charl was there too."

"I don't give a damn about Charl! You're different. I need you."

"Why?"

"Why?" Her voice rose as she echoed the question. "How big a fool are you that you can't guess that? Who else on this ship can I turn to? Who—Earl!"

"Stay away from me!" He backed as she came towards him, arms extended in open invitation. "Dephine!"

Her bare arms fell to her naked sides, the slap of her palms clear in the hold. Stripped she stood beneath the UV lights, taking her turn at the prophylactic precaution. One which Dumarest doubted would be of much use but at least it had a psychological benefit.

"All right, Earl," she said, bleakly. "So I mustn't touch you. But at least you can look at me. Does it help?"

She was like a child, he thought, wanting confirmation of her charm. A small girl asking strangers if they thought she was beautiful. But there was nothing childish about her body, lean and lithe though it was. The breasts and hips were those of a mature and feminine woman. The clear musculature revealed beneath the skin added to rather than distracted from her appeal. There was life in her, a vibrant urge to experience it to the full, a heat of primeval passion. One which had abruptly revealed itself when she'd heard the news as if nature itself was trying to compensate for imminent death by a burst of biological activity. An urge he had recognised and felt even as he had denied its logical outcome.

Death could be riding on his hands—he must not pass it on.

"Give yourself thirty minutes," he ordered. "Then call Allia to take your place. Make her strip if you can."

"That's impossible, Earl."

"Try, but don't touch her. Don't touch anyone or anything unless you have to."

She turned, slowly, arms lifted above her head in order to accentuate the thrust of her breasts, stomach indrawn. Her legs, long and slender, looked like marble as she stood on her toes.

"Am I beautiful, Earl?"

"Beautiful."

"You mean that?"

He said, bluntly, "Of us all you will look the best in a coffin. Don't fall in love with yourself so deeply as to forget that. Thirty minutes, remember, not a second less."

Charl Tao called to him as Dumarest passed the door of his cabin. He sat, a bottle of unusual design on the table before him, glasses to hand.

"Earl, come and join me."

"You know better than that, Charl."

"We were both with Fren and if one of us has contacted the disease then so has the other. We were both exposed. Which isn't to say that either of us needs to suffer. Sit and I will explain."

The man had medical experience and what he said was true. Dumarest entered the cabin. He sat and watched as the plump man tilted the opened bottle. The wine was of a thick consistency as if it were syrup, but in the mouth it had a clean sweetness filled with stinging bubbles.

Charl smiled at his expression. "Unusual isn't it, Earl? A rare and precious vintage made on a small world which has nothing to commend it aside from this one art. One day, perhaps, I shall go back to it and obtain a vinery. All it needs is money and a gracious presence. You would have no difficulty in obtaining a place in their society."

"Have I money?"

"Did I say you had? The vines are passed from mother to daughter and from a part of her dowry. To obtain a footing it is necessary to marry. Money makes a man more attractive but some, attractive without, could make themselves an easy living." He lifted the bottle and poured a little more into Dumarest's glass. "A wine which lasts, Earl. A little goes a long way."

"Like trouble."

"And disease. You've experienced it before?"

Dumarest nodded, remembering a settlement, the cries of the afflicted, the deaths, the plague which had swept through the camp like a wind. He had survived with a few others and had walked away leaving the place in flames; rude huts and gathered branches making a cleansing pyre for the dead.

"And?"

"Buboes beneath the armpits. Rashes. Pustules on the face, neck and body. Nothing like this. You know of it?"

"No." Charl sipped at his wine. "It is most probably a mutation, something triggered to sudden life which feeds on an unsuspected weakness. The ebon patches seem to have some resemblance to gangrene though I can see no true correlation. Certainly they are foci of destroyed and expelled tissue."

"Not origin-points?"

"I don't think so. I studied Fren pretty closely as you know. The first blotch was the forerunner of several more all of which appeared in rapid succession. They begin as pin-points and expand within the course of a few hours, the red rim becomes noticeable only when they have reached an easily visible diameter. Help yourself to more wine if you want it, Earl."

"I have enough. A virus?"

"Most probably, yes."

If so their chances were small. In the closed environment of the ship it would be quickly spread from one to the other, most probably had been spread already. Dumarest remembered the stripped cabin of the dead steward; the bulkheads had remained, the air he had breathed, the things he had touched.

"How is Fren?"

"Unconscious. I've kept him that way though I will admit we could learn more if he were revived. As it is I've taken smears and done what I could, but without instruments it isn't enough. We haven't even a microscope. There is no centrifuge, no laboratory equipment, no reagents. All I managed to do was test growth-rates on a culture plate and try a few inhibiting chemicals." Charl lifted his glass, sipped, puffed his cheeks to accommodate the dancing bubbles. "What medicines do we have?"

"Some sedatives, tranquilizers and pain-killers," said Dumarest.

"Slow-time?"

"No."

"A pity. If we'd had some we could have fitted our patient with intravenous feeding and given him a month's subjective living in a day. At least it would have shown us the progression of the disease."

Dumarest shrugged. The question was academic. Slow-time, the reverse of quick-time, was expensive and not to be expected in the medical stores of a ship like the *Varden*. And there was little point in accelerating a man's metabolism to a high factor unless they had the equipment to make it worthwhile.

"Talking of time," said Charl. "The Captain's changed our course, right?"

"Yes."

"And lengthened our journey by how long?"

"Does it matter?"

"It could, Earl. To some of us it could mean life itself." Charl lifted his glass in a toast. "To luck! May it attend us! And to a pleasant journey—it could be the last any of us may take!"

The handler collapsed two days later, falling across the chess board and scattering pieces to either side. The engineer backed away, his face betraying his fear, making no effort to help as Dumarest tugged at the limp figure.

"Get hold," he snapped. "Lift him. Carry him to his bunk."

"No! He's got it!"

"You've been facing him, breathing his air, touching the same pieces as he did. Help me with him—you've nothing to lose." Dumarest straightened as the man still hesitated. "I asked you to help," he said tightly. "Now I'm not asking, I'm telling you what to do. Get this man to his bunk."

"And if I don't?" The engineer scowled as steel flashed in Dumarest's hand. "You'd cut me, is that it? You'd use that knife. Well, mister, two can play at that game."

A rod stood in a tool rack, a long, curved bar used to ease the generator on its mountings in case of adjustment or repair. A thing too long for easy handling, but deadly in its potential. The engineer tore it free, lifted it, sent it whining towards Dumarest's head. Ducking he felt the wind of its passage stir his hair. As the engineer lifted the bar for a second blow Dumarest darted in, smashing his fist against the engineer's jaw, sending him staggering back. He struck again, his fist weighed with the hilt of the knife, bringing down the blade so that the point pricked the skin of one cheek.

"I'm not playing. Start anything like that again and I'll finish it."

"You—"

"Pick him up. Move!"

The handler was in a bad condition. He breathed with difficulty, chest heaving, throat swollen, face covered with sweat. Dumarest slashed open his tunic with his knife, the reason he had drawn it in the first place. A gesture the engineer had misunderstood.

From where he stood at the cabin door the man said, "How bad is he?"

"Bad enough. Do you know if he's allergic to anything?" Dumarest frowned at the negative answer. "What has he been eating lately?"

"Some fish we had in cans."

"Did you eat the same?"

"No, I don't like fish." The engineer leaned forward. "Is that what's wrong with him? Bad food?"

It was barely possible, but one symptom could be masking another. Fabric parted as Dumarest ran the edge of his knife down the undershirt and exposed the naked chest. It was adorned with a suggestive tattoo, writhing lines and smears of color which made it difficult to see the actual state of the skin.

Impatiently he sliced through the belt and bared the stomach. It was covered with minute ebon blotches.

"Two down and seven to go," said Charl Tao when he heard the news. "A lucky number, Earl. Seven is supposed to hold a special significance. It has magical properties and is the number of the openings to the body; two ears, two nostrils, a mouth, the anus and the urethra." He ended, dully, "I learned that at school."

Information of no value. Dumarest crossed the floor of the salon and helped himself to a cup of basic from the spigot. It was a thick liquid, laced with vitamins, heavy with protein, sickly with glucose. A single cup would provide a spaceman with sufficient energy for a day.

"Aside from the significance of numbers have you learned anything else?"

"Little. The steward would have been in close contact with Harmond. It was part of his job to aid him in small ways. And he was a close friend of the handler."

Which meant that both would have been exposed early to the disease. In that case it was to be expected that both should fall sick before the others.

"The incubation period?"

"It's anyone's guess, Earl." Charl lifted hands and shoulders in a shrug. "A few days, at least, but how many is impossible to tell. I simply haven't the data. And it could vary with each individual. Harmond may have succumbed quickly because of the infection present from his wound. It would have lowered his resistance. The handler was probably the first to be contaminated."

But he wasn't the first to die. Fren Harmond did that, his life slipping away as he lay locked in drugged unconsciousness. Dumarest wrapped the body in plastic, heaved the dead man, his bedding, all he had owned in the way of clothing to the evacuation port. Grimly he watched as the apparatus cycled, lamps flashing as the contents of the cubicle were blasted into the void.

A man dead who would probably have still been alive if they hadn't left Hoghan as they had.

One who would at least have had a chance.

On the *Varden* there was no chance. The ship held no vaccines, no medicines, no skilled aid. No instruments to determine the nature of the invisible killer. Nothing to give a clue as to how it could be defeated. Survival now depended strictly on the make-up of the individual: the strength of resistance-factors, antibiotic generation, the ability to combat the virus, to meet the challenge, to live.

A gamble in which none knew their chances and could only guess at the odds.

Allia Mertrony rocked back on her heels from where she knelt before the polished disc, her head buzzing, echoes ringing in her ears, the pounding of her heart a clenched fist beating within her chest. Before her incense rose in coiling plumes, the last of her supply. No matter, it had been enough. Her prayers had been answered. Lars, long dead and long waiting, had stirred and sent her a message.

He was waiting. He was impatient. When would she come? And God too was waiting.

But long to be in his presence as she did, the Prime Directive must be obeyed. To live while it was possible. To extend existence until it could be extended no further. Then, and only then, could she join Lars and go to her reward.

To die. To rest. Suicide was forbidden and though old she had no ills. But the joy of life had long since left her and, aside from prayer, she lived but to sleep and eat. Fear had gone now that she had been reassured. Her faith was strong.

And good deeds remained to be done.

"Mad!" Charl Tao shook his head as he entered the salon. Nodding to Dumarest and Dephine he drew basic, sipped, made a face, then forced it down.

"Who is mad? Me?" Dephine stared her anger. "I'm fed up with being cooped in a cabin. All right, so it's crazy to mix, but what difference does it make now?"

"None," he said mildly. "But I wasn't talking about you, my dear. I was talking about the old woman. She's turned into a nurse. I left her washing the handler, tending him, crooning like a mother over a child."

"How is he?"

"Fever high. Profuse sweating which is to be expected at such a temperature. Headaches, shivers, pains in the joints." Charl added, slowly, "He's also delirious."

Dephine said, sharply, "Raving, you mean?"

"By now he must be far gone in hallucination. The crisis, I think. Either he will begin to recover in the next few hours or he will die."

"The warning symptoms," said Dumarest. "Have you isolated them yet?"

"I can make a guess, Earl, no more. The handler complained of headaches and nausea a day before he collapsed. However he had been drinking heavily and so the symptoms could have had another cause. But a few hours before he was stricken he did complain of double-vision. It could mean nothing, Earl."

Dumarest said, quietly, "You're wrong, Charl. The engineer complained of that very thing when I saw him last. He also said he felt sick. I told him to lie down and try and get some sleep. If we find blotches on him—"

They were scattered over his shoulders and upper torso, flecks like blackheads which would grow into ebon flowers rimmed with scarlet.

"Help me!" His hands lifted, groping. "My eyes! I can't see! Help me!"

Charl straightened from his examination and shook his head, baffled.

"The eyes don't seem to be affected, but without instruments I can't be sure. And even then my experience is too limited to arrive at a conclusion. A part of incipient hallucination, perhaps? A psychosomatic syndrome?"

"How so?"

"See no evil therefore it doesn't exist. See no illness and it cannot threaten. An escape from unpleasant reality. Was he afraid?"

Dumarest nodded, looking about the cabin, seeing the garish pictures pasted to the bulkheads. Colorful depictions of longed-for pleasures, exaggerated interwindings of shapely limbs, scenes of a vague, dream-like unreality. Visible proof that the engineer had not only imagination but an earthy mind. An imagination which had now turned against him, magnifying his pain.

As the man groaned Dumarest felt a sudden chill, the touch of something against which he had no conscious defence. An enemy which naked steel could neither cow nor defeat. A thing as intangible as a thought, as destructive as a fanatic's ambition.

"I burn!" The engineer writhed in a paroxysm of agony, twisting on the bunk, rearing, his back bent like a bow, hands clenched until the nails dug into his palms. "The pain! Dear God, the pain!"

"Another variable, Earl." Charl shook his head in baffled irritation. "His sensory apparatus appears to have been affected. Usually in men of his type the pain level is inordinately high but now it seems to have been lowered to an incredible extent."

"Could the virus be generating some form of nerve-poison?"

"How can I tell? It's possible in which case it would account for the sudden onset of pain. There hasn't been time for extensive tissue-damage. But if that is the case then why weren't the others affected in the same way?"

"Maybe they were," said Dumarest. "Harmond was drugged until he died, remember?"

"And the handler could be suffering as much in his delirium as the engineer in his physical anguish." Charl nodded, his eyes thoughtful. "In each case it is obvious that the sensory apparatus has been affected by the virus and it could be mere chance which dictates the course the disease will take. If others are affected they could either go insane or—" He winced as the engineer screamed again, a hoarse, rasping, animal-like sound. "Earl!"

The screaming died as Dumarest fired drugs into the tormented body. He checked the load of the hypogun as the engineer sank into merciful oblivion. It had taken a heavy dose—too heavy if it was to be maintained. The supply of drugs was limited and the more he took the less there would be for others.

If others came to need it? If they did and none was available?

Dumarest looked at his hands thinking of Dephine.

Chapter Seven

————◆————

The lamps flashed, the port cycled, Allia Mertrony went to meet her God. A small, aged, withered woman who had spent the last few days of her life bringing ease to others. Standing before the port, Dumarest hoped she would find what she had sought. Hoped even more that never again would he have to void the shell of a human being into space.

That never again would he have to watch a woman die.

The lights were too bright, hurting his eyes and misting his vision so that in dancing haloes he saw again the thin, shrunken features, the ugly blotches, the eyes, the final radiant smile. Her faith had been strong and she had died happy. Now she would drift for eternity or be drawn by gravitational attraction into a sun and disintegrate in a final puff of glory. A minute flame which would, perhaps, warm some future flower, grace some unknown sky.

Fanciful imagery which had no place in a ship which had become a living tomb.

Tiredly Dumarest walked from the port and through the vessel, a journey he had made too often now. Harmond had been the first, then the engineer closely followed by the handler, then the old woman. He frowned, trying to remember how many were left. Four? Five? Five—but for how long?

He stumbled and saved himself from falling by catching at the bulkhead, breathing deeply for a moment before straightening and continuing the journey. Fatigue robbed his limbs of strength and caused his joints to ache. Too many days without sleep, too many screams to be quelled with the diminishing store of drugs. Charl Tao had helped but now he lay supine on his bunk, glazed eyes staring at the ceiling of his cabin, drugged with his own compounds, ebon flowers blooming on his face and chest and hands.

Haw Mayna was insane.

He sat cross-legged on the deck of the salon, a lamp burning before him, a sliver of steel in his hand. A thin-bladed knife which he heated to redness in the flame and then held firm against the blotches which marked his naked body.

Each touch accompanied by the smoke and stench of burning meat.

The shriek of agony which, in his madness, had become the scream of his defiance.

"Earl!" Dephine stood beside the door, turning as Dumarest entered the compartment. "He's crazy. Raving mad. Do something."

"What?"

"Knock him out. Drug him. Anything."

"He's a man," said Dumarest. "And he knows what he's doing."

"Burning himself?"

"Ridding himself of corruption." Dumarest watched as the tip of the knife grew red, smoke rising from the burned tissue adhering to the steel. "Who knows, it may work. Nothing else seems to."

Mayna's scream drowned her answer.

"Leave him."

"How can we, Earl? He should be restrained. Who can tell what he might do?"

Dumarest stared at the woman, recognising her real concern. The navigator, in delirium, could run wild, loosing his distorted fancies on the delicate construction of the vessel, destroying the sensors, the delicate guidance mechanisms on which they all depended. Which, if ruined, would leave them all to drift endlessly in a metal coffin.

"He has to be restrained, Earl. If you haven't the drugs then take care of him in some other way. Kill him if you have to, but make sure he remains quiet."

"Kill him?"

"Why not?"

"Are you forgetting he's a sick man?"

"No, Earl, I'm not forgetting." Her teeth gleamed white beneath her upraised lip. "And I'm not forgetting a man on

Hoghan. Your comrade—but you didn't hesitate then so why hesitate now?"

"And if you were like him?" Dumarest met her eyes. "If you were sick and ill and needing help would you want me to be your executioner?"

"If there were no other way, Earl—yes." She frowned as Mayna screamed again. "At least lock him in so he can do no harm."

Dumarest stooped as he closed the panel, lowering his head; raising it as the momentary nausea passed. He saw the look of concern on Dephine's face and wiped the sweat from his eyes.

"Earl?"

"I'll be all right." And then, as she made to touch him, "Don't do that!"

"Why not? What the hell difference does it make now? You're sick, Earl. You look all in. At least come and rest for a while."

"Later. Go and see how Charl is getting on. I've work to do."

"Earl?"

"Do it!" he snapped. "Just do it!"

He stood watching as she moved away, trying not to yield to the sudden weakness which assailed him, the pain which clawed at every muscle.

The control room was locked. Dumarest pounded at the door, kicked it, then slipping the knife from his belt rammed the sharp steel between the edge and the jamb, levering until the latch snapped and the panel swung open.

From the interior gloom Remille said, "Take one step over the edge and I'll burn you down."

"Captain?"

"You heard what I said, Earl. I mean it." The voice was thick over the rustle of heavy movement, the captain moving in his chair. "Just stay away from me."

"I must know—are you sick?"

"What the hell could you do about it if I am?"

"Are you?"

"What the hell do you think?" Remille's voice was bitter. "My ship rotten with disease, my crew dead or insane, passengers evicted—yes, I'm sick. Sick of the years of struggle

I've spent and all for what? Quarantine and penalties and my ship lost and that's if I'm lucky. And if I'm not—"

"You'll die," said Dumarest. "Is that what you want?"

Remille made no answer, breathing heavily. A point of light shifted as he moved, a momentary brilliance which vanished to reappear again as he blinked an eye. A sudden flurry of activity from the tell-tales and Dumarest saw his face, strained and tense, the lifted hand and the laser it held, the finger hard against the trigger.

"I'm not coming in," he said quickly. "I just want to talk."

His knife was in his hand, a throw and the captain would be dead. But he was limned against the light and no man, no matter how fast his reflexes, could lift a blade, aim it, throw it with accuracy in less time than it took for another to move his finger. The captain might die, but Dumarest knew that he would die with him. And he had no intention of killing.

"To talk," he said again. "You know the situation. Mayna's gone insane."

"I know."

"Then what about the course? Did he set it and feed it into the computer or was he running it from his head?"

"You're asking do I need him anymore," said Remille. "The answer is no. I don't need him, but you need me. If you've any fancy ideas about taking over the *Varden*, forget them. It's my ship. If it goes then I go with it."

"And if you go?" Dumarest waited; then, when he received no answer said, "I've saved some of the drugs, Captain. Enough to put you into a casket. You could ride Low until we reach our destination. A time-trigger could be set and—"

"No."

"You'd wake and be able to make a landing. It would give you a chance. Even if you have the disease they might be able to cure you. Life, Captain. Think of it."

"Is that what you came here to talk about?"

"Yes."

"Then you've wasted your time. I'm not leaving the control room. If you want to freeze yourself then go ahead, but you're not going to freeze me."

"But—"

"Get out! I mean it, Earl, get the hell away from me. I'd rather not shoot but I will if I have to." The heavy voice broke, the sound of breathing harsh in the gloom. "Leave me, damn you! Leave me—and don't come back!"

The corridor spun as Dumarest stepped back from the control room. He turned, almost falling against the bulkhead, feeling the hard metal beneath his hands. He rested his forehead on it, leaning forward as sweat ran from his face to drip on the deck. A sudden flood of perspiration born of the tide of pain which rose to engulf him, a searing, acid-like fire which turned every nerve into a channel of torment.

Dimly he heard the slam of a panel, smelt the scent of burning metal. The laser welding shut the control room door. If he was to die Remille intended to die alone.

Dumarest drew air into his lungs and slowly straightened. His head ached and he felt a little dizzy but the pain had lessened a little as if the very fury of its onslaught had numbed feeling. He took three steps down the passage, cannoned into a wall, took three more and almost fell. Grimly he regained his balance. As if from a far distance he heard Mayna scream. Another echoed it, closer to hand.

"Earl! My God, Earl!"

Dephine! He waved her back as she came running towards him, her figure seeming to expand and diminish in his sight.

"No! Don't touch me!"

She said, angrily, "Earl, you fool, you're not thinking straight. What are you going to do? Join Mayna? Lie on the deck here and die? Stop being so damned noble and get some sense. Now lean on me and let's get you to a bunk. Damn you, Earl! Do as I say!"

It was easier to obey than argue and the return of pain made it impossible to resist the arm she threw around him, the pull which drew his own over her shoulder. Twice she had to halt as he doubled, retching, blood running down his chin from bitten lips. Blood which dripped on a hand and made tiny flecks of red among the ebon blotches which mottled his skin.

"You've got it," she whispered. "Earl, you've got the disease. God help me now!"

Once, as a young boy, Dumarest had torn the nail from a toe during a chase after game and, alone, had had to hobble for miles over rough and stoney ground. The pain then had been something he had imagined would never be equalled, but now the memory of it was a pleasantry against the agony which suffused every cell of his being.

Pain which seemed to escalate, wave after wave each more intense than the last, a ladder of agony on which his diminishing consciousness rode like a cork on water, bobbing, turning, writhing as he desperately tried to escape. A wound would have brought blood-loss and the attendant shock with its mercy of oblivion, but the thing which had turned each nerve into a hyper-sensitive conductor of pain had, as yet, done no irrepairable damage to his physique. And, alone, pain does not kill.

"Earl!" A faint voice echoing from across unimaginable distances. *"Earl!"*

A touch and a lessening of anguish, a chance to breathe without searing torment afflicting the lungs, to move without the muscle-tearing agony of cramps. To look upward and see, haloed in a nimbus of light, a mass of red hair.

Hair which shifted and shimmered and moved as if with a life of its own.

Hair which turned to the color of flame.

"Kalin!"

"Kalin? No, Earl, it is I, Dephine." A mumble, echoes vastly magnified, words which boomed and rolled and became thunder. And then became words again. *"What can I do? More drugs? Dear God, guide me, what can I do?"*

Words which turned into a susurration, a thin whisper, the scrape of a nail on slate, a pain in itself so that he rolled and tried to close his ears and saw, painted on the inside of his eyelids, images which spun and turned and lunged towards him to stand and become familiar.

A face, gibbering, falling back with the hilt of a knife protruding like a growth from the orbit of an eye. An old woman nodded, her eyes like insects, smoke rising to veil the space between them. A burst of gargantuan laughter.

"Earth? Earth? Where is Earth?"

A scream which continued, a rawness of the throat, an ache in the lungs. Light and flashing fire and, again, the halo of red hair limned against a blur of white.

Delirium.

Dumarest sank like a stone into the escape of hallucinations, illusions; the over-strained fabric of his mind running from the intolerable prison of his flesh. Pain alone does not kill. He could not find the surcease of death. He could no longer bear the relentless agony.

Only madness was left.

Madness and memory.

He was in a place of shifting patterns of light with strange shapes moving in wild abandon, cones and spheres, polyhedrons and cubes, constructs of lace and squat forms which teased the eye with varying contours. A medley of jumbled impressions; sensory stimuli received and registered by a brain which had lost the ability to distinguish illusion from reality. Pictures drawn from the storehouse of memory and thrown against his consciousness as slides projected against a screen.

Death was there, waiting as it had waited all his life; closer now, more avid to clutch and claim him for its own. A black edging to the picture and one which dulled the bright colors of happy anticipation. An edging which turned scarlet, which congested into a profusion of lines, took on a hatedly familiar aspect.

Became the Seal of the Cyclan.

Faces wreathed in scarlet hoods, all alike in their skeletal aspect, skin taut over bone, heads shaven, eyes deep-set, mouths lipless; only the burning intelligence in the sockets of the skulls giving evidence of life and dedication. Cybers, men dedicated to the organisation to which they belonged. Living robots of flesh and blood, incapable of feeling emotion, knowing only the mental pleasure of intellectual achievement.

Hunters!

And he was their quarry. Chased from world to world, always having to anticipate where they would be next, how they would strike. Not to kill—had that been their aim he would have long since been dead, but to take. To hold. To question. To wring from him the secret he carried. The gift of Kalin.

Kalin with the hair like flame!

"Earl! My hands! Let go!"

A well of darkness into which he sank, stars flashing, dying, replaced by others burning with transient glory, a scatter of gems lying on the black velvet of a cosmic jeweler. Stars which formed patterns each the symbol of a biological unit. Fifteen units which, correctly assembled, would form the affinity twin. The artificial biological construct which

could be either dominant or submissive according to the re-
versal of one of the units forming the chain. Injected into
the bloodstream the symbiote would nestle in the cortex and
intermesh with the central nervous system. The ego of a host
would be diminished, reduced to a sleeping node while that
of the dominant partner would take its place. The effect
was to provide a new body for the master-half of the twin. A
surrogate which became an actual extension of the ego. By
its use an old man could become young in an alternate body,
an old woman regain her beauty. A bribe none could resist.

"Earl! Tell me about Kalin. Kalin, Earl, tell me about her."

A voice like the wind, formless, disembodied, a thing to
be ignored in the pursuit of bitter memory and yet enough
to guide the direction of thought.

Kalin who had succumbed to temptation. And who, in
the end, had given him the formula stolen from a secret
laboratory of the Cyclan.

A secret they had to regain.

A thing which would accelerate their domination of the
galaxy, their aim and ambition. Once they had it every ruler
and person of influence would become an extension of their
organisation, the mind of the cyber residing in a new body,
moving it as a puppet, making it their own.

Incredible power, and the Cyclan would move worlds to
regain what they had lost: the secret sequence of the units
forming the chain.

"Earl?"

Dumarest moved, fretful, images dissolving and being replaced by new. A horde of men busy at work, an entire
planet devoted to a single aim. Workers of the Cyclan busy
trying to resolve the combination, but mathematics was
against them. The total of all possible combinations of fifteen units was high. Even if they could make and test one
every second it would take them four thousand years to
cover them all.

"Earl! For God's sake answer me! Earl!"

The voice again, louder, demanding, imperious. A thunder
in his ears. Dumarest forced open his eyes, they were matted
with dried pus, the lids heavy, the light streaming through
them a red-hot sword plunging into his brain.

"Wa—" He tried again, mouth and lips refusing to respond, his tongue a puffed and cracked mass of raw tissue.
"Water . . . give me water."

It flooded over his lips and chin, made wetness on his naked chest. With the liquid gurgling came the voice, rising, breaking.

"Thank God, Earl! Oh, thank God! I was so afraid. Earl! Keep living, my darling. Keep living!"

"How. . . long. . ."

"Days. Days and days. Don't go away again. Stay with me, Earl. Don't get delirious again. Stay sane, damn you! I need you! Stay sane!"

A voice like a whip, the lash cutting through the fog, the terror he heard in it, the fear a stimulus to exert his strength. It was barely enough for him to keep his eyes open, to form words.

"Water. Give me more water."

A shadow and a seeming deluge which filled his mouth and pressed into his lungs. Coughing he expelled it, a spray which lifted like a fountain, glittering droplets falling like jewels. Dimly he was aware of his nudity, of the stickiness of his body, its heat and aching discomfort and, above all, the fatigue.

"Tired," he mumbled. "Tired."

"Earl! Stay alive, Earl! Live!"

He would try but it was hard to think and impossible to remain alert. His eyes closed and, in the darkness, Dumarest felt himself slipping back into the safe, warm haven he had constructed in his mind as a defence against pain. A warren into which he would mentally crawl to suffer the grinding ache of disorientation.

The last thing he consciously heard was the harsh sound of a woman's tears.

Chapter Eight

The room was a jewel carved from an emerald, the light soft through windows with tinted panes, the coloring of walls and floor matching that of the ceiling, the furnishings a variety of kindred shades. From the bed Dumarest looked at it, ran his hands over silken covers shimmering with the delicate hue of early petals. Green, a restful color, one designed to alleviate fear. He knew he must be in a hospital.

"Welcome to the living." A man stepped from behind the head of the bed where he had stood out of Dumarest's field of vision. He was slender, of medium height, his face smooth and his voice gentle. He wore a uniform of dull green adorned with silver patches on shoulders and cuffs. "A jest, but you must forgive me. Before you ask this world is Shallah and you are in the Hammanrad Institute. My name is Doctor Chi Moulmein. Yours?" He nodded as Dumarest gave it. "At least you have no doubt as to your identity. And you came from Hoghan, correct?"

"Yes. How—"

"All in good time." Smiling the doctor lifted a hand. "Let me say at once that you have made a remarkable recovery. Even the fittest of men usually take a few minutes to gain complete orientation after such a long period of unconsciousness, but you became almost immediately aware." He gestured towards a panel which stood attached to the coils and pipes of a mass of complicated apparatus. "Again, my congratulations."

"For what? Living?"

"For having the will to survive. Without it your recovery would have been impossible. Chelha is not the most gentle of plagues. However you have nothing to fear now. One at-

72

tack makes you immune if you survive it and you can be released from quarantine when you wish."

Dumarest looked at the man, the assembled apparatus.

"How long?"

"Six months subjective, fifteen days actual. Slow-time, of course, but the treatment had to be interrupted to permit recovery, checking and essential tests. We used the Rhadgen-Hartle technique of maintaining unconsciousness by the use of micro-currents applied directly to the sleep centers of the brain. Perhaps you are aware of it?"

"Under a different name, yes."

"Of course, but the RH method does have some advantages over the usual application and we are rather proud of it. A system of induced electronic shocks which maintain the flexibility and power of the musculature," he explained. "The patient wakes with no trace of the expected weakness and can resume an active life without delay. You will have noticed that you are not hungry. A further benefit; the stomach has been nurtured on a diet of selected roughage and concentrated staples. This, in addition to normal intravenous feeding, ensures a minimum of fat-loss and tissue-wastage. I bore you?"

"No."

"It is my specialty, you understand and, to be frank, I was pleased at the opportunity of using it for so long a period at a stretch. It will probably be advisable for you to spend a few days doing certain exercises, mainly for the restoration of full coordination and automatic responses. This, of course, will be your decision. Now, as to how you came here. You are curious, am I correct?"

Dumarest nodded.

"A signal was received from your vessel and a ship was sent to intercept and rescue. Messages had been received from Hoghan warning of the outbreak of plague and so all precautions were at hand ready to be taken. You were sealed, brought down to planet, installed in the Institute and taken care of. A lucky escape, sir, if I may say so. Not one in a hundred can hope to recover from Chelha and not more than one in ten thousand is naturally immune."

Luck, and it was still riding with him. Dumarest looked at the room, the expensive appointments, the mass of complicated equipment. Money, time, and care had been spent on him—who was footing the bill? And what had happened to Dephine?

Both questions were answered at the same time.

"Your lady is taking care of everything, sir. She is a most remarkable woman and, in fact, she saved your life. A natural immune which is rare enough, but one with intelligence and knowledge also. She realised that, unaided, you would not survive the crisis and remembered a fragment of learning gained when she studied elementary medicine. You would know about that, naturally, but she would have needed a grim determination to have carried out her decision. A bold woman, sir, and a brave one. May I congratulate you a third time on your choice of a partner."

Dumarest said, patiently, "You will excuse me if I seem dull, but I wasn't conscious at the time, as you must know. Just what did she do?"

"To save you?" The doctor shrugged. "She could not, of course, have known that she was a natural immune but as time passed and she didn't contact the plague she must have had an inclination that she was in some way favored. The problem was how to pass her resistance-factor to you. Without the correct equipment she could not make a true vaccine and it was essential that the appropriate antibiotics should be transmitted active and alive. I am not using professional terminology, you understand."

"Get on with it, man. What did she do?"

"If the flesh is seared a blister will form," said the man a little stiffly. "The blister will contain a fluid which is derived from the blood, containing none of the potentially harmful corpuscles but a kind of strained and refined distillation which can be used as an innoculation-fluid. This is what your lady did."

"Burned herself?"

"On the breast and thigh. Both wounds are now fully healed and, naturally, there are no scars." The doctor made a small gesture as of a man suddenly reminded of something. "She is well and, like yourself, out of quarantine. I'm sorry, I should have mentioned that before. Naturally you would have been worried."

"Naturally," said Dumarest, dryly. "Where is she now?"

"At this time of day most probably at the Krhan Display. You wish to join her?"

Dumarest said, "Get me my clothes."

The Institute itself stood on a rolling expanse of close-cropped sward; the building housing the display was set in an oasis of flowers, giant blooms which held within their petals the blended colors of broken rainbows. The breeze was blowing towards him and Dumarest caught their scent long before he reached the flowers themselves. The odor was sweetly rich, stimulating to the nostrils, yet holding within itself the cloying stench of decay. The petals too were thick and curled like segments of tissue and, as he headed towards the path, some of the great blooms turned to follow his progress.

"My lord?" A guard blocked his path, eyes roving over Dumarest from head to foot. He wore his own clothes, refurbished, the plastic glistening with a liquid sheen, the grey in strong contrast to the profusion of color. Like himself they had been cleansed, checked, passed fit for normal circulation.

"My lord?" said the guard again, the title more a question than a deferential politeness. "May I be of assistance?"

"The Lady Dephine?"

"She is within." The guard gestured towards the curved entrance of the display. "And you? A patient? My apologies, but—" He broke off, a little discomforted. Those who could afford the expense of the Institute were not usually so sombre in their choice of dress. "To the left as you enter, my lord. The lady is probably in the inner chamber."

Music echoed with faint tinklings as Dumarest passed through the door, an electronic chime activated by his body-mass, serving both to announce his presence and to warn those within that a stranger had come to join them. A peculiarity for which he could see no need, as there had seemed none for the guard. Then, as he looked through the shadowed gloom, the reason became obvious.

The walls glowed with color, patches of flaming brilliance interspersed with areas of muted luminescence, a profusion of sparkles and shades, of glows and shafts and points, of pulses and ripples in each and every combination of hue. Works of art constructed of metal and crystal, of trapped gasses and seething liquids, of sponge-like ceramics and foils which hummed and moved as if alive.

Before one a woman stood, lost in rapture, her hands squeezing her naked breasts, her breathing a deep and quickening susurration. Beyond her a man crouched in an attitude of attack, lips drawn back over snarling teeth, hands lifted, fingers hooked, ropes of muscle standing clear on his naked arms and torso. A couple lost in each other, so interlocked that it seemed as if they were one. A young girl who simpered and ran to stand with her thumb in her mouth and invitation in her eyes. An oldster who drooled. A matron who stood with parted lips and cried in silence. A boy who talked to the air in muted gibberish.

Dumarest passed them all, his boots soundless on the padded floor, light from the display shimmering from his sterile clothing, the polished boots, the hilt of the knife riding above the right.

Dephine was in the inner chamber.

She sat on a circular couch which slowly turned in the centre of the floor so that one seated could see the entire extent of the inner display. It was in sharp contrast to that outside, sombre tones now instead of stimulating brilliance, lines and planes holding a subtle disquiet which seemed to darken the glowing constructs. Her eyes were blank, emerald pools which glistened with reflected light beneath the carefully dressed mane of her hair. Eyes which blinked and became alive when Dumarest stood before her.

"Earl!" She rose, hands lifted, the nails glowing as they turned to rest the palms against his cheeks. "Earl! At last!"

"You've been waiting long?"

"An eternity! Earl, you look so well!" Her palms stroked his cheeks, ran down the line of his jaw, the tips of her fingers resting on his lips, following the contours of his mouth. Her eyes were wide, luminous with unshed tears of joy, her face bearing the radiance of a young girl. "Earl"

A sudden flood of natural emotion or a reaction to his presence caused by the effects of the display? Dumarest stepped back, looking at her, conscious of the impact of her femininity, his own wakening desire.

"Dephine, you look well."

An understatement, she looked beautiful. Rich fabrics clothed the long, lithe contours of her body, gems shone at ears and neck, wrists and fingers. More from the auburn cloud of her hair. Her eyes gleamed beneath the slanted brows and, in the hollows of her cheeks beneath the prominent bone, luminous shadows danced to enhance the wide invitation of her mouth.

He said, a little unsteadily, "Let's get out of here."

"Why, don't you like it?" Sitting she patted the couch at her side. "Join me, Earl. Let me feel the warmth of your body close to mine. The life that is within you. The strong, so strong determination to survive. The only reason you are with me now. Did they tell you that when you woke? That a lesser man would have succumbed?"

"This place—"

"A work of genius, Earl. Krhan was a master of his art. A visionary who took inert material and imbued it with life." Her voice sobered a little. "He haunted the beds of the dying and recorded their every hope and fear and aspiration later to use those recordings to program the structure of the artifacts which now rest all around us. Extremes of emotion caught and reflected to be assimilated by those who come here to stand and concentrate and become one with the emanations. You've seen them, Earl, you understand."

Auto-hypnosis which stripped away layers of inhibition and released secrets, desires and aspirations. And here within the inner chamber?

"The culmination of his art, Earl," she said when he asked. "Sit and watch for long enough and time ceases to have meaning. Death is robbed of its terror. Life becomes a pulsing surge of demand. Life, Earl, and emotion, and the desperate hopes of those who have left their desires too late and, in dying, sent them to blaze in a final burst of emotive appeal. Do it now, Earl. Can't you grasp the message? Do it now before it is too late. Do it! Do it!" Her arms engulfed him, holding him with a desperate yearning, her body radiating a demanding heat. "Do it, Earl! Damn you, do it now!"

A bird descended with a flutter of wings to land on the fleshy petal of a flower, to peck, to whirr into the air again. A free creature of the air, protected in this environment, a thing of grace and beauty.

As she watched it fly away Dephine said, "We need to talk, Earl."

He nodded, looking back at the building housing the Krhan Display. A trap set among riotous flowers, its insidious attraction as subtle as the scent emitted by the bloom of a carnivorous plant. To it would come the ambulatory patients of the Institute eager to taste the new excitement, experience the new thrills. To stand and release inhibitions and act the parts transmitted by those who had died, taken and adapted by the artist. To indulge in stimulated passion. To be watched by skeins of glowing luminescence.

To return again and again, drawn by the depictions as a moth is drawn to flame.

"How long?"

"Have I been waiting? Days, Earl, almost a week now. They had to check me out under slow-time. You needed specialised treatment—but you know all that." She looked back at the massed flowers, the building with its rounded roof. "The Krhan Display beguiled me. It was a way to pass the time. It holds truth, Earl."

"No. Dreams, illusions."

"The truth," she insisted. "How many die eaten with the regret of lost opportunities? The fury of having waited too long? Of building for a future which, for them, no longer exists? Do it now, Earl. A fact which life has taught me. A truth among others." Her voice grew hard. "So many others."

Too many, perhaps, and some of them only a facet of the truth she imagined she had gained. Glimpses of reality distorted by false imagery and garnished by faded tinsel; the lure of promised excitement too often turning sour. How often had she known disappointment? How often had she reached for a new thrill, a new experience, another adventure? How many layers of defensive protection shielded the real woman?

A path led to a bench ringed with scented shrubs and he led the way to it, sitting, waiting for her to settle.

"What happened, Dephine?"

"On the ship?"

"Yes. . . the others?"

"Charl died by his own hand. I went in to him and he pleaded with me to give him his compounds. One of them must have contained poison."

"Mayna?"

"Dead too."

"How?"

"Does it matter, Earl?" She refused to meet his eyes. "He died, that's all you need to know. His screams were driving me crazy and—" She broke off. "Forget it."

A knife plunged into the heart, the impact of a club against temple or spine, drugs to distort the metabolism, there were many ways to kill a man.

Dumarest said, "Remille wanted to be alone. How did you talk him into landing?"

"I didn't. He made a recording and set the computer to throw the ship into orbit. They picked up the appeal and came up to see what was wrong. Remille was dead. They sent the vessel into a collision-course with the sun and brought us both to the Institute." She added, bleakly, "I think they would have sent us with the ship if I hadn't been able to pay."

The jewels they had found in the loot—the answer to the expensive treatment which had saved his life.

Dumarest said, sincerely, "Thank you, Dephine."

"For what?"

"Doing what you could to save me. The doctor told me about the burns. Without those innoculations I wouldn't be alive now."

"No, Earl, you wouldn't."

"And so I thank you."

"You thank me," she said, dryly. "Is that all? A few words quickly spoken?" And then, as he made no comment, added, "If so it isn't enough. I want more, Earl. A lot more."

"There is little I can give," said Dumarest evenly. "But you have the jewels and can retain most of my share."

"It still isn't enough."

Simple greed? He doubted it, but had to be sure. "What then?"

Her answer was direct. "You, Earl. I want you."

Marriage? In the display they had been governed by passion, riding a tide of sensual pleasure, of desire, of lust. She had been wild in her abandon, surrendering all restraint, concerned only with their union and careless as to who might be watching. An abandon he had shared in an explosive release of primeval energy. There had been words in the glowing dimness, things whispered in the language of lovers. Terms of endearment, protestations of affection, promises which he had heard from other women and which he had learned to discount—when passion died such things were often forgotten. And, influenced by Krhan's genius, neither had been wholly normal.

"Earl?"

She expected an answer, but he delayed giving it, letting the silence grow as he studied the lines of her face. It was hard, cold, a tiny muscle twitching at the corner of her mouth. Her nails made little scratching sounds as they rasped over the rich fabric of her gown.

Not the face of a woman declaring her love to a potential mate. But if not marriage then what?

"You're cold," she said at last. "Had I said that to another man he would have leapt to the obvious and be talking of our future life together. Especially after what happened between us in the display. Yet you say nothing. Why, Earl? Am I so repulsive?"

"Say what you mean, Dephine."

"Cold and hard and direct." She looked down at her hands as if reluctant to meet his eyes. "You're an unusual man, Earl, but I knew that before we left Hoghan. And in the *Varden* you proved it again and again. The *Varden*—how can I ever forget it? Days spent with death all around, not knowing if I would contract the disease, not even knowing if Remille had sent the ship to plunge into a sun. Can you imagine it, Earl? Can you?"

The cold glare of light and a silence broken only by moans and screams of the sick and insane. Alone in a ship which had become a tomb, the air tainted with the stench of burning flesh, filled with the restless mutters of nightmare.

"It's over now," he said. "Over."

"Yes, Earl. A danger passed and a problem solved and for you that is the end of it. You will move on, visit other worlds, meet other women, but you don't carry, as I do, the curse of your heritage. I had thought myself rid of it, but in the *Varden,* and later when I felt the impact of Krhan's genius—Earl, it isn't easy to forget the past."

"Can you ever, Dephine?"

She caught the sombre note in his voice and with an impulsive gesture reached out a hand and touched the side of his face. A touch which turned into a caress as her fingers moved softly over his cheek, to rest on his lips, to lift and be pressed against her own. A kiss by proxy; a thing often done in taverns by harlots with eyes as hard as the metal which graced their nails. But this was no tavern but a bench set among scented bushes and the woman was regal in self-assured pride.

A pride which crumpled as, tremulously, she said, "Earl! I need you! Please don't make me beg!"

"Need me for what?"

"For your strength, your courage, your skill. Because

you are a man in every sense of the word. Because I am
afraid."

"Afraid?"

She said, dully, "I belong to an old and honored family.
One so steeped in tradition that it has become a way of life.
Can you understand that? To live by a code which must not
be broken. Of pride which can admit of no weakness. Of
reputation which must be maintained no matter what the
cost. I was a rebel and when the chance came to escape
I took it. Since then I have done many things." Light glittered
as she lifted her hands and looked at her nails. "Things which
could be regarded as having sullied the good name of my
House."

"So?"

"I want to go back, Earl. I want to go home. Yet how
can I be sure of a welcome? I could be challenged—there
is nothing so cruel as outraged pride. So you see why I
need you. I must have a champion. A man to stand at my
side and to shield me with his strength. Just for a while,
Earl, until I am accepted, then you can go your own way if
you want."

She had tended him and saved his life—he couldn't refuse.

"Very well, Dephine," he said. "I'll take you home."

Chapter Nine

Home was Emijar, a small world lying at the edge of a dust cloud, the solitary planet of a dying sun. From his balcony Dumarest studied it, looking at the distant loom of hills, the rolling swell of terrain. From below came the sound of voices and, leaning over the parapet, he could see small and colorful figures busy driving horned beasts from pasture into stalls for milking. Boys at their labors as the girls would be hard at work spinning and weaving. The children of the Family learning the essential disciplines of husbandry.

With his elbows leaning on the carved and weathered stone Dumarest examined the exterior of the house. It was a big, rambling structure which had grown over the years, yet the new additions had blended with the old adding to instead of detracting from the original conception. The tower in which he stood reared towards the sky, walls enclosed small courtyards and the thick, outer walls were topped with crenellations. A house which was a combination of farm and fortress. A building which had stretched to embrace generations of residents as it had expanded to contain the accumulation of centuries.

A place of dust and cobwebs, invisible, intangible, but there just the same.

Dumarest straightened and turned and stepped back into the room he had been given. It was shaped like a wedge, the floor of polished wood, the ceiling thick with massive beams, the walls softened by an arras of brightly decorated fabric. The bed was wide and covered with a quilt stuffed with feathers. A chest stood at its foot and a low table at its side held wine in a crystal decanter together with two goblets. The door was of solid wood, barred with metal straps and thick with the heads of nails.

A knock and it opened.

The man standing outside said, "My apologies if I have disturbed you. Am I permitted to enter?"

"Do so."

"You are most kind, Earl. I have neglected you, an unforgivable lapse, but I crave your indulgence. The excitement of Dephine's arrival—you understand?"

"I think so."

"To return after so many years!" The man made an expressive gesture. "An event which must be celebrated. Already word has been sent to all members of the Family. But I am remiss. You are comfortable? The room is to your liking? You have bathed?"

Dumarest nodded, studying his visitor. Hendaza de Monterale Keturah was Dephine's uncle, a man of late middle-age, his short, stocky body clothed in sombre fabrics, his tunic alone bright with the encrustation of colorful badges. Symbols of achievement and rank, Dumarest knew. As important to the man as the holstered weapon he carried at his waist, the firearm no adult would ever be seen without.

Dumarest said, flatly, "How is Dephine? Has she been accepted?"

"By me, certainly, but I have traveled in my youth and know that tolerance is a part of civilized living. Others are less generous, but they will be won over given time and, if the worst should happen, well, she has her champion."

A calm acceptance of his role as if it were the most natural thing in the world which, in this society, it was. Dumarest stepped back towards the window and stared in the direction of the city and the spacefield, fifty miles to the west. A distance which had been covered by a raft in as many minutes. The sun was low, the smokey red of the mottled disc dazzling.

As he turned, blinking, Hendaza said, "Earl, how much did Dephine tell you? You are close to her, I know, the fact that you are her champion proves it. But how deeply did she confide in you?" And then, as if part of a ritual formula, he added, "If my words offend you I apologise. If the apology is insufficient then I am at your disposal."

To participate in a duel, a ritual combat in which right

was assumed to triumph. A thing in keeping with the great house with its invisible cobwebs of ancient tradition which insisted on careful attention to minute detail.

"You don't offend me," said Dumarest. "She told me very little."

Little of importance, at least, though much which had to do with promises and what he would expect to find on Emijar. A small trader had finally brought them to her home world, the third vessel they had taken since leaving Shallah, tiresome journeys with tedious breaks as they waited for connections. Days in which they had talked and nights devoted to passion.

"A strange and wilful girl," mused Hendaza. "Even when but a child she had a wild streak in her which made her object to discipline. Yet how can civilization survive without a firm basis of rules and customs? Each must know his place and each must maintain both pride and position. Perhaps you have met similar cultures in your travels?"

"Similar," said Dumarest. Static societies doomed to fall apart beneath the impact of new ways, but he said nothing of that. "When will Dephine be fully accepted?"

"After dinner tonight those who wish to object will be given their chance, but it will be a formality I'm sure. What to do now? Some wine? A little exercise? A tour of the House? Come, Earl, let me show you around. There are others you should meet; Lekhard for one, Kanjuk and young Navalok should amuse you." His laughter was a dry rustle of contempt. "We shall find him in the chapel."

It was a dim place filled with shadows, the gloom dispelled at points by the glow of vigil lights. They rested beneath a collection of broken weapons and, in the faint light from the floating wicks, the things seemed to move, to shift as if gripped by unseen hands.

As Dumarest paused in the doorway he saw a thicker clot of shadow, a form which rose from where it knelt, turning to reveal a white and drawn face, a pair of staring, luminous eyes.

"Navalok de Monterale Keturah," said Hendaza with a sneer. "One day, perhaps, he could rule the House—if he ever finds the guts to win his trophy."

The rite to prove his manhood, the beast he would have

to kill before he could claim adult status. A barbarism in keeping with all the rest.

Dumarest called, softly, "Navalok? Come and talk to me. Come, boy, I won't hurt you."

"Do you think I am afraid of that?" The boy stepped forward, limping a little, his lips tightly compressed. He was young, barely reaching to Dumarest's shoulder, and thin with a stringy leanness which could result from malnutrition or the long, flat muscles of a natural athlete. In the gloom his eyes were enormous, the starting eyes of a helpless beast which knows that it is trapped and can see no way of escape.

"A wise man is always wary of strangers," said Dumarest. "It is caution, not fear. A thing I learned years ago when I was just a boy. And you, Navalok? How old are you?"

From where he stood Hendaza said, spitefully, "Long past the age when he should have become a man, Earl. He is of my blood but I have to say it. You talk to a coward."

And listen to a fool. Dumarest said, mildly, "Could you leave us, Hendaza? I'd like to look around a little. Navalok can guide me if he agrees."

"He will agree." Hendaza glowered at the boy. "This is Earl Dumarest. An honored guest. You will remember that."

"My lord?" Dumarest waited as Hendaza left them alone. "Will you guide me?"

"Yes, of course, but there is no need of titles."

"From either side," said Dumarest. "Now, what have you to show me?"

Together they walked slowly down the length of the building. The floor was flagged with stone and the sound of the youth's footsteps made a dull resonance from the vaulted roof.

"Tell me about these relics." Dumarest gestured to the items illuminated by the soft glow of the vigil lights. "They are relics, aren't they? Things kept from the past?"

The boy halted before a shattered sword.

"Arbane used this against an olcept ten times his own weight. It ripped his stomach and brought him down but he managed to kill it and return with the trophy before he died."

"And this?"

A broken spear with much the same history. The weapon used by a man who had killed and later died from injuries received while killing. The list lengthened, the young voice rising a little as he warmed with his stories, the names and deeds of those he envied rolling from his tongue.

Brane who had walked on bloodied feet to hurl his trophy before the Shrine. Tromos who had hopped. Kolarz who had crawled. Arnup who had lost an arm and used his teeth and single hand to support his burden. Sirene who with both legs shattered and one eye gone had writhed like a snail leaving a slime of his own blood and intestines.

Tales of blood and suffering, of the will overcoming the limitations of the flesh, a saga of those who had struggled and won the coveted prize and who had died with fame and honor. Men who had wasted their lives to leave nothing but broken weapons and distorted memories, but Dumarest said nothing of that.

"You see, Earl," said the youth, "It isn't enough just to kill. The trophy must be carried back to the Shrine."

"Is that essential for those who hope to rule?"

"Yes. A man must prove himself. Some go after a normal trophy and leave it at the Shrine and are content to rest on their proven courage. Others, especially those in direct descent from the Elder of the House, must gain a trophy accepted by all as one fit for the position they wish to hold. Nothing less than seven times the weight of a man."

Dumarest said, "Can you show me what an olcept looks like?"

The picture gave no indication of size and the colors were too garish to be true, but something of the ferocity of the creature had been captured and set on the pane of painted glass. A long body upheld by four, claw-tipped legs. A knobbed tail. A head consisting mostly of slavering jaw with grasping appendages to either side. Horns which curled like upraised daggers. Fur and scale and spines of bone. A composite of bird and reptile with something of the insect blended with the mammal.

"The dominant life-form of this world when the early settlers arrived," said the boy. "Much blood was spilled and many Families broken before they were beaten back into the mountains. Now they have learned to leave us alone but, at times, they swarm and destroy crops and fields, buildings and beasts in a wave of destruction. Nothing can stop them aside from the massed fire of heavy weapons. Usually all that can be done is to remain safe behind stone."

Dumarest remembered the massive stone walls, the towers

and crenellations. It had been no accident that the house had adopted the features of both farm and fortress.

"Why aren't they hunted?"

"They are. Their heads provide the trophies."

Small beasts relatively easy to kill yet each destroyed made the flock that much less of a hazard. A necessity incorporated into the social structure and used for a double purpose. A triple purpose when it came to deciding the fitness of those aspiring to rule.

The women, of course, would be helped and even given kills to call their own. Then Dumarest remembered Dephine, her savage determination, her almost feral heat in anger and love. Such a woman would scorn such aid and she could not be alone. Here the females were equal to their men.

"And the Shrine?"

It lay behind the chapel, an echoing chamber flagged with blocks of red and yellow, lights glowing like stars on the marble walls, small points gathered thickly before the arched opening and the inner chamber. Within it rested a slab of polished obsidian the surface cluttered with a variety of objects; a book, some instruments, a chronometer, the injector of an engine, the plastic leaves of a record-file, a spool of thread, a jeweled toy, a dozen other items.

"From the First Families," said Navalok reverently. "Each placed here some object of personal value and, by these things, they are remembered. Each House, of course, has its Shrine, for all hold the Firsts in veneration. As we hold those of us who sit in the Hall of Dreams."

Ancestor-worship coupled with a primitive rite of puberty added to the rigid traditions and codes of a ritualised way of existence. Once of value for the culture to survive, perhaps now a lead weight dragging it to oblivion.

"You sit in the chapel," said Dumarest. "And you pray for strength, the ability to be like those you respect and admire. The heroes whose weapons you guard and whose exploits you remember. Yes?"

"Of course, Earl."

"Why?"

Navalok frowned. "I don't understand. I am weak and you must have noticed the way I drag my foot. An accident when I was a child, but it has left me deformed. How can I hope to gain a trophy without the help of those best suited to give it?"

"They are dead, Navalok." Dumarest was patient, the conditioning of a lifetime could not be eliminated by a few words. And to deride would be to arouse a reactive antagonism. "They are dead," he said again. "All of them."

"But they gained their triumph."

"And died doing it. Is that much of a success? Wouldn't the achievement be greater had they returned unscathed to hurl their trophies before the Shrine?" Dumarest smiled as he posed the question, his voice deliberately casual. "In my experience the man who remains unscarred after a fight is the one to be feared, not the one displaying his lack of skill."

For a moment, watching the play of emotion over the young face, he thought that he had gone too far too fast. Only a fool could have missed the implication and no one likes to be told that his heroes were stupid rather than brave. Then, as Navalok opened his mouth to reply the air shook to the deep and solemn note of a bell.

"The curfew," he explained. "The gates are now closed and the House sealed for the night. Soon it will be time for dinner, Earl. It would be best for us to part now and get ready."

Dinner was held in the great hall and was obviously the high point of the day. Dumarest joined the throng of guests standing before the tall, double-doors, his grey tunic in sharp contrast to the others adorned as they were with a plentitude of badges. Even the women wore similar symbols, stars fixed to sashes draped over one shoulder and, like the men, they were armed.

"Earl!" Hendaza came bustling through the assembly two others at his heels. "Allow me to introduce you to those whom I mentioned. Earl Dumarest, Lekhard de Monterale. Lekhard, this is—"

"I know who he is." The man smiled with a twist of his thin lips. Young, arrogant, he radiated an aura of self-assurance. His tunic was a blaze of ornamented badges. "We both know, eh, Kanjuk?"

Hendaza said, stiffly, "I take offence at your attitude, Lekhard."

"So you take offence." The man shrugged. "If you want satisfaction it can be arranged. The usual place when the bell tolls at dawn?"

"No." His companion, a tall man with a smooth face and enigmatic eyes, rested a gemmed hand on the other's sleeve. Like Hendaza he was of middle-age. "This is no cause for a quarrel, Lekhard. You were rude to interrupt and Hendaza was right to remind you of your lack of manners. We do not want our guest to think we are barbarians."

"Does it matter what a stranger thinks?" Lekhard's eyes roved over Dumarest's plain tunic, halted at his weaponless belt, dropped to stare at the hilt of the knife thrust into his boot.

"Yes, my friend, Dumarest is armed." Kanjuk smiled as if at a private jest. "You were slow to notice that. Now that you can accept him as an equal we can act like civilized men. You have visited many worlds, Earl?"

"I have."

"And seen many cultures, no doubt. Have you met other societies like our own?"

"As yet I have seen little of it."

"And so have no evidence on which to judge. Well, time will cure that. I would like—" He broke off as trumpets sounded from the doors which now swung open. "It is time we went in to dinner. Later I would appreciate the chance of resuming this conversation. Lekhard! To me!"

Kanjuk raised a hand as he moved off into the throng now streaming through the opened doors. At his side Hendaza said, "Head for the upper tables, Earl. You sit next to Dephine. As her champion it is your right."

She smiled as he took his place, reaching across the space between them to touch his arm, gemmed fire winking from her fingers. She was resplendent in a gown of embroidered fabric, the sash draped over her shoulder bright with badges, the pistol at her belt resting in a holster of gilded leather.

"You are happy, Earl?"

"I am here. Just what I am supposed to be doing is something else."

"You are my champion." Her fingers gently scratched the back of his hand. "With all that implies. But don't let appearances deceive you. On Emijar men can smile as they murder and murder as they smile."

Dumarest shrugged away his hand from beneath her nails, not bothering to probe her meaning. Instead he studied the great hall and the assembly it contained. All the Family, it seemed, had come to welcome Dephine. They sat at long, narrow tables set on the stone floor, each loaded with a variety of foods and wines. At the lower end of the hall, separated a little from the others, were the tables occupied by those who had yet to win their trophy. Social inferiors not as yet regarded as having the right to an opinion.

Navalok was among them, his face sombre as he picked at his food.

Dumarest reached for a fruit with a golden rind and lifted it from where it rested on a mat of leaves. The skin broke beneath his fingers to release a flood of sickly sweet juice. The flesh was tart, slightly acid, dissolving to a chewable mass of fibre.

At his side a man said, "So far no challenges, but there is time yet before the final bell."

"You expect one?"

"I? No, but who can tell what is in other minds?" The man sipped a little wine. "If any should come Alorcene will do his best to negate them. Dephine was always his favorite."

"Alorcene?"

"Keeper of the Scrolls." The man gestured towards the highest table. "Ah, there he is. I thought he wouldn't leave it much longer."

The sharp note of a bell sounded above the hum of conversation and, as silence fell, an old man lifted his hand.

"According to ancient tradition and with the will of those who guide the destiny of this noble House let all listen and pay heed. To this place has returned the Lady Dephine de Monterale Keturah. Of those present do any deny her right to remain? To rejoin the Family? To resume her rightful place among us? If so speak that all may hear."

Dumarest reached for another fruit. The episode was a ritual at one with the rest and a part of the ceremony he had been warned to expect. The public announcement, the avowal of intent, the opportunity for those who held old grievances to have them aired. Nothing would come of it, or so Dephine had sworn. His very presence would take care of that.

Again the ring of the bell, the solemn intonation.

From a table lower down the hall a woman rose and said, clearly, "I deny her right. She left under a cloud. There was a suspicion of theft."

"Full reparation has been made. Thrice the sum involved has been returned to the injured party. Forgiveness has been granted and no animosity is now borne. Do you wish to challenge?"

"If reparation has been made—no."

The bell sounded again as the woman sat, the third and last time for any present to object.

Dumarest narrowed his eyes at a flurry from the far end of the hall. From the doors a man strode with an arrogant impatience towards the upper table. A tall man, his scarred face edged with a ruff of beard. One who wore a tunic heavy with badges. One who had timed his entrance well.

Halting he shouted, "I am Galbrene de Allivarre Keturah. I accuse this woman of theft, of lies, of harlotry. Of breaking her word and of ignoring her promise. I say she is a disgrace to the Family. A vileness which should be erased. I challenge her!"

Chapter Ten

The room was flanked with alcoves each containing a sculptured form; the cold eyes of depicted men and women staring blindly at the group around the table. In its center rested a lamp of glowing crystal, streamers of red and yellow, blue and emerald, azure and dusky violet painting shifting hues on the stone, the faces and clothes of those gathered.

"Galbrene," said Dephine bitterly. "The fool. Who would have thought he'd nursed a grudge for so long?"

"His pride—"

"To hell with his pride!" She glared at Hendaza, cutting him short, careless of any affront. "Why wasn't he stopped? I had your word there would be no trouble and now this. A public challenge and one that can't be settled privately. Or can it? Lekhard?"

"Even if he would agree it would be difficult," he said, flatly. "And it is unthinkable that he will agree. A public challenge must be met and be seen to be met. If not his own honor will carry the taint and suspicion of cowardice."

"Kanjuk?"

"My dear, what can we do?" The man spread his hands in a gesture of resignation. "Galbrene will not be denied. And it isn't a matter of a personal insult which could be settled with due regard to form yet without real danger to life. He has claimed you insulted the House and, I must tell you, there are many who agree with him. An unfortunate occurrence, but one which cannot be either ignored or dismissed."

Dumarest said, "Why not?"

It was the first time he had spoken since the dinner had ended and those present had gathered in the room. Beyond

92

the doors men and women milled in anticipation, the air filled with the hum of speculation. A hum which held a feral sound, a savagery he had heard before.

One underlying the rasp of naked steel, the harsh panting, the thud of feet in the ring where men faced each other with bared knives and fought to the death. Blood and pain to titillate a watching crowd. Wounds and death to provide a spectacle for the jaded and bored. Dumarest remembered the burn of edged steel, the warmth of spilled blood, the shock of pain, the stench of fear. Remembered too the sudden expression in the eyes of an opponent as his own blade had driven home. The stunned, incredible realization that, for him, life had ended.

"What?" Lekhard turned with a lithe, animal-like movement, a wash of blood-red light painting his features, a mask from which his eyes glittered like jewels. "What are you saying?"

"I asked a question," said Dumarest evenly. "In my experience most things can be settled in more than one way."

"You don't understand," said Kanjuk. "On Emijar there is only one way to settle such an insult and all know it. The challenge must be met."

"Without armor," added Lekhard. His tongue caressed his lower lip. "Surely you have knowledge of our customs?"

A society which lived on the edge of violence—the guns carried were not toys. Yet to avoid the escalation of feuds certain rules had been evolved. Duels were fought with the contestants wearing armor which limited the vulnerable area. Limbs could be broken and painful wounds received, but the possibility of actual death was slight. The victor gained a badge from the vanquished, a token scalp, and the more obtained the greater the admiration.

But a public challenge such as had been made to Dephine would be to the death.

She said, forceably, "It must be stopped. Earl, you cannot fight the man."

"He must!" Hendaza looked from one to the other. His eyes were determined. "As your champion, Dephine, he can't refuse."

"He can and must!"

"No!" Lekhard was as determined as the other. "For one thing to refuse would be to gain the derision of the House. That you could, perhaps, bear. But there would be more.

The gauntlet, for one. And for your champion—" he made
the word a sneer "—well, we do not treat cowards lightly
on Emijar. Such men are taken and left unarmed in the
haunts of the olcept. None have ever returned."

Dumarest said, "Dephine, just what does Galbrene have
against you?"

In the following silence he looked from one to the other,
seeing each trying to avoid his eyes, each masking his face
in his own way; Lekhard with a sneer, Kanjuk with a bland
expression, Hendaza with a frown. Only the woman was
outright.

"Once, Earl, years ago now, I promised to marry him."

"And now he wants to kill you?"

"Yes."

"An odd way of showing his love."

"Love has nothing to do with it, Earl. Even the word itself doesn't mean to him what it does to you. It is a matter
of pride. He chose me and I rejected him. I broke my given
word. I made him a mockery in the eyes of his companions. If
he could that man would tear me apart with his bare hands."
Pausing she added, "I'm sorry Earl. I didn't know this would
happen. If—" She broke off as Alorcene entered the room.

He crossed to the table, sat, his face expressionless. His
hands, in the colored streams of light, looked like scraps of
paper or thinly scraped bone as they rested before him.
Hands which matched the thin dryness of his voice, quiet
now in startling contrast to what it had been in the hall.

"I have questioned Galbrene de Allivarre Keturah and his
claim is just. He has the right to challenge. You, Dephine de
Monterale Keturah, have only the right to defend either in
person or by use of a champion."

Dumarest said, "Her life at stake for a broken promise?"

"It is our way," said the old man quietly. "But it is not
her life at stake but her reputation. Should you fall she will
be ostracized, scorned, disavowed. She will be expelled from
the House, the Family, from this world. But you, Earl
Dumarest—you will be dead."

Through the uncurtained window he could see the stars,
a glitter of distant suns each with its own worlds, their
pattern broken by the sprawling blotch of an interstellar
dust cloud, its edges haloed with a faint luminescence. From

the balcony could be seen the night-shrouded land, the distant hills a wavering, ghostly line in the cold glow of the heavens. Beneath the parapet lay sheer stone, more in an unbroken expanse for twenty feet above, the wall ending in the overhang of a peaked roof. Things he had spotted in the fading daylight, barriers now augmented by the sealed portal, the watchful guards on walls and roofs.

A precaution against external enemies but one which kept men in as well as out.

Lying supine on the wide bed Dumarest stretched, easing muscle and sinew, his thoughts busy with odd scraps of assembled information.

The Shrine—would the items it contained hold any information as to the whereabouts of Earth? If the First Families had landed here long enough ago it was barely possible that an old navigational table would give the coordinates he had searched for for so long. Would Navalok permit him to search? A good start had been made to win his friendship, but more could be needed. The boy was a dreamer, one cursed by having been born to the wrong society at the wrong time. Earlier he would have been quietly disposed of so as not to contaminate the gene pool with his undesirable characteristics. Later he could make a place for himself as a thinker, a poet or an artist, a planner or a teacher. Now he was caught between two fires, tearing himself apart with the desire to prove himself according to the customs of his Family yet lacking the physical attributes which would make it possible.

But he would try and, trying, he would die.

Dumarest turned, thinking of his own problems.

An hour after the great bell sounded at dawn he would have to fight and, from what he had seen of Galbrene, the man was no stranger to combat. The badges he wore proved that, each a trophy of victory as the gun he carried showed his courage against the olcept. And, as Lekhard had pointed out, the man had not been satisfied with a minor kill. He had gone after bigger game and Dumarest knew what it took to face a ravening beast with nothing but a scrap of edged and pointed steel.

He heard the knock and had risen and was at the door before it could come again. The passage outside was lit with a smokey yellow light which gleamed from the gems set in the mane of auburn hair.

"Earl?" Dephine glanced at the naked blade in his hand. "Did you expect an assassin?"

"Get inside." He closed the door after her, thrusting home the thick, wooden latch. "What do you want?"

"To talk. I couldn't sleep and I missed you." Her eyes met his as she tilted back her head. "A light?"

The curtains rasped from their rings as he drew the thick material across the panes. An unnecessary precaution, perhaps, but it was late and curiosity could be aroused. For a second he fumbled in the gloom then, as light blazed from the lamp, Dephine came towards him, arms extended.

"Earl!"

He ignored the invitation.

"Galbrene was a surprise," he said, dryly. "One I could have done without. Could there be others?"

"I didn't know, Earl," she said, quickly. "I told you that. It shouldn't have happened and, on any other world, it wouldn't have mattered. He could have been taken care of without all this ridiculous formality."

"On any other world it wouldn't have been necessary." Dumarest watched as she poured wine. "Theft, lies and harlotry," he murmured. "How long ago was it, Dephine? Eight years? Ten? Twelve?"

"Why?"

"Galbrene has either a long memory or you made a hell of an impression."

"Both." She met his eyes without smiling and deliberately drank some wine. "Do you want me to pretend that I'm a pure little innocent who didn't know what she was doing? All right, so I'm guilty of everything he accuses me of, but so what? Are you any better? A killer? A man who lives by violence? Have you any right to judge?"

"Have I judged?"

"No," she admitted. "You haven't. Not from the very first. You took me for what I was, but treated me as if I were all the things a man hopes to find in a woman. Not as a cheap whore or a thief or a liar or someone who should have known better. Not like these fools who look at me and then at you and decide it would pay them to keep a shut mouth. You, Earl—you're a man!"

"Tell me about Galbrene."

"What is there to tell? He wanted me and, yes, we were betrothed. It was an arrangement and one of the reasons I wanted to get away. And I stole also, that I admit, but I needed money for passage and other things. And I didn't know that I'd ever want to come back. I didn't know that until after I'd met you and then, in the ship, with death all around and you lying so ill, dying I thought—Earl, if I'd known how to pray I'd have done it then! Prayed for you to live and to love me as I love you. To want to be with me so that we could find happiness together. To build a home, Earl. A home!"

The dream of every wanderer of space; to find a woman who would look at him with love in her eyes, to have a place to call his own, to rear children, to put an end to loneliness.

Yet his home was not here. It had to be on Earth—if he could find it.

He watched as she turned away from him and drank the rest of her wine. His own he left untouched and she looked at it then to where he stood.

"Earl?"

"I asked about Galbrene."

"To hell with him! I've told you—"

"Nothing of importance," he said coldly. "I want to know how he thinks, how he feels, the way he gets himself ready for action. Has he a weakness which could be exploited? What is his strength?"

"I don't know, Earl," she admitted. "It's been too long and, anyway, his tactics might have changed. He's older now. Anyway, what does it matter? You can beat him. You can take him in any way you want. Just keep him moving and—"

"He'll fall in my lap?" Dumarest shook his head. "If you think that then you're a fool. No fight is ever certain. Always there is the unknown factor. No man is invincible no matter what he thinks. Or," he added grimly, "what others might like to think. He could win, Dephine, remember that."

For a moment she stared at him, wide-eyed, then turned to pour wine, the neck of the decanter rattling against the rim of her glass.

"Earl, you mustn't die! You musn't."

He smiled at her intensity.

"I mean it, damn you!" She threw the glass of wine to one side, coming to stand before him, hands resting on his shoulders. "No matter how you do it, Earl, you must live. Life has so much to offer when this is over. I'll be fully accepted and we could marry and settle on land to the south or close to the field if you'd prefer it. We'll have money enough to live comfortably. Enough to support children, Earl. Children!"

Her voice, her body, held temptation. There was strength in her and fire and a beauty which belonged more to the wild than to the conglomerations of civilisation. A temptation which she enhanced as her arms lifted to wreath his neck, the full warmth of her body pressing against him with familiar urgency.

"Earl!" she whispered. "Earl, my love! My love!"

A fighter who dallied with women before a bout was a fool. Gently Dumarest pushed her away.

"Goodnight, Dephine."

"Earl? You—"

"Goodnight."

Dawn broke with a flood of color, streamers of red and orange, russet and gold, amber and strands of purple which hung like gaudy banners in the sky. Banners matched by the pennants surrounding the combat-area, the bright badges worn by the spectators on tunics and sashes.

The stands were packed but there was no jostling, no voices raised in argument and Dumarest knew why. An armed society is a polite one; when a look or word can bring injury or death then neither are lightly given. And surrounded by people ready to gun down anyone killing without cause an aggressor was forced to have regard for the code.

Hendaza said, "You have no doubts as to the procedure, Earl? If there is anything you need to know don't hesitate to ask. As your official mentor and aide it is my duty to help you in any way I can."

He had done his best, arriving an hour before dawn, fussing as Dumarest had bathed, worried at the little he had eaten. Now he stood at his side in the opening leading to the arena—a courtyard ringed with rising tiers of stone which served as seats. In another opening across the empty space Galbrene would be waiting.

Dumarest said, in order to please the man, "Are all challenges fought like this?"

"Not exactly. We stand as you are now but we are armed. Pistols—and the first one down or hit yields the day. We walk at the signal and fire at will." He rubbed at his chin, perturbed, torn with conflicting loyalties. Dumarest was a stranger, Galbrene was not, yet he liked Dephine despite what she had done.

"But all serious challenges are to the death?"

"Yes."

"And if the victor should decide to be merciful?"

"I don't know." Hendaza frowned. "I don't think it has ever happened. But if—"

The blast of a trumpet drowned what he was saying.

A second note and the ritual began.

Dumarest stepped forward, seeing the shift of shadow in the far opening, the sudden appearance of a man. Like himself Galbrene was naked aside from abbreviated shorts. His hair was freshly cropped and his beard was little more than a fuzz the shorn hair offering little chance of a hold. Oil shone on his body so that little gleams of reflection accentuated the firm musculature beneath the skin. Ropes and ridges of muscle packed with animal-like power. The body of a man who had dedicated his life to the pursuit of physical perfection.

Dumarest slowed a little, feeling the coolness of sand beneath his feet, the firmness of stone beneath the layer of grit spread to ensure good traction. Galbrene walked a little wide-legged, the result of the bulging muscle padding the inside of his thighs. His arms too were lifted away from his body, thick biceps and massive forearms ending in broad, splayed hands and fingers.

Dumarest could understand Hendaza's shocked incredulity when he had demanded they meet without weapons.

"But, Earl, you can't! It would be madness!"

The man had wanted him to fight with pistols—but that would have given Galbrene the advantage. He had used guns all his life. A knife would have given Dumarest a better chance, but to demand one weapon was to open the door to an alternative demand. The whole point of the code was that the opponents should be as equal as possible, the only way to ensure that right would triumph.

And so they were to fight almost naked and hand to hand.

"Fool!" snapped Galbrene as they came closer. "Why waste your life on such a harlot? Yield now and I will be merciful."

Dumarest hesitated, appearing to consider the offer, noting the slight bunching of the toes of Galbrene's right foot, the swing of his left arm.

"If it can be made to look good I'm willing," he said. "I didn't expect anything like this. Dephine—"

He broke off as Galbrene charged, stooping, taking the rasp of a bunched fist over his shoulder, twisting and feeling the slamming blow of a foot against his side. His own hand grabbed at the ankle, slipped on the oil, rose with a stiffened edge to hit hard behind the calf. He had tried for the knee but it had been beyond reach. Deliberately he made the blow weak.

They broke and circled, hands lifted, feet sidling on the sand. Again Galbrene rushed in, hands pummelling, a knee jerking upwards, his head lowering in a butt to the face. Dumarest moved to one side, dodged the knee, took a blow on the upper arm, sent his own clenched fist rising upwards to pulp the tissue of the nose.

"Fast!" Galbrene dashed blood from his lip with a sweep of his hand. "You move like a greased olcept. But how long can you keep it up?"

Longer than if he wasted breath in talk. Dumarest backed, dodged as the other rushed again, wove from the reaching hands and struck twice at a bicep. Blows which could have been delivered to the air for all the damage they seemed to have done.

"Fast but weak!" Galbrene laughed. "And you claim to be a champion? Dephine could have done better. Too bad, my friend, but now you die!"

A quick end to the combat and a greater enhancing of his own prowess. A mistake, one Dumarest had helped him to make. Galbrene, confident of his own physical superiority, had forgotten the danger of guile.

Dumarest dropped as hands reached towards him, spinning to one side, his hand grabbing up a mass of sand, stinging grains which he threw into the other's narrowed eyes. As the cloud of grit wreathed Galbrene's head he rose, hands poised, the edges like blunted axes as they struck at the point where the neck joins the body. Blows which would have broken an ordinary man's neck, ruptured arteries and sensitive tissue. Blows which met solid muscle which did not yield.

Dumarest felt a fist drive into his stomach, another scrape the edge of his jaw. Excited, unthinking, Galbrene pressed forward, eager to pound, to pulp, to destroy. His massive fists were like hammers which beat and beat as if he were a smith working at an anvil. Blood from his broken nose ran unheeded over his face to smear his chest and dapple the sand with carmine stains.

Dumarest ran. He turned and raced over the sand, to halt, to run again as like an engine of destruction Galbrene pounded after him. A race to gain time, a retreat in order to clear his head of the flashing stars the other's fists had created. Movement to wear the other down a little, to rob his blood of needed oxygen.

A small gain, but in the arena small gains could spell the difference between victory and defeat.

"Slow down!" yelled Galbrene. "Stand and fight like a man!"

A demand echoed from the stands where men and women leaned forward, shouting, faces avid, eyes reflecting their hunger. The lust for blood and pain and death, the primeval desire always to be found when the veneer of civilization was torn away and the true nature of the beast was revealed.

"Kill! Kill! Kill!"

The shouts were like the beat of a drum, a command to Galbrene, one which spurred him on to gain even greater fame than he possessed. The weakness of the culture to which he belonged; a society which insisted that a man always needed to prove himself without end.

"Kill!"

Dumarest halted, turned, ducked as the arms came towards him to rise within their circle, his hands stabbing upward with stiffened fingers, hitting the soft flesh beneath the chin, the windpipe and larynx. As the arms locked around his torso he swept his hands up and back, sent them forward to stab at the eyes. The left missed, the fingers catching the heavy brow to slip upwards to the cropped hair. The right plunged home, turned the eye into a thing of ruptured tissue and oozing fluids, sent blood to gush over the cheek and shoulder as, too late, Galbrene jerked his head to one side.

"Kill!"

Hurt, the man was still dangerous, the more so because of his pain. Dumarest felt the arms tighten and struck again at the neck, the remaining eye. Galbrene, eager to save his sight, leaned back, his arms slackening a little and Dumarest ducked, rammed the top of his head beneath the other's chin, jerked down his elbows and, resting his hands on Galbrene's shoulders, lifted his feet and slammed them hard against the point where the thighs joined the body.

A move which, had it worked, would have torn him from the crushing constriction of the arms.

One which failed.

Galbrene snarled, moved, and Dumarest felt his feet slip from the oiled skin. He settled them again on the other's insteps, his own arms circling the thick torso, fingers interlocking, the muscles of back, shoulders, thighs and loins straining as he fought the pressure which threatened to splinter his ribs and drive the jagged ends into his lungs. The constriction which, unless stopped, would snap his spine like a rotten twig.

"Kill!" The shouting was another thunder to add to the roar in his ears. "Kill!"

Galbrene was strong, but his head was being bent backwards and his back arched as he yielded to the pressure. A loss of leverage which alone was saving Dumarest's life. One which the other could regain by throwing himself down, twisting free his head, using his legs and massive arms to their full advantage.

Dumarest felt him shift, felt a foot slip from where it rested, the other as Galbrene jerked back his legs, sensed the coming jerk which would free the trapped head. Releasing the grip of his arms he sagged, turned limp as if stricken and then, as Galbrene shifted his own grip and moved his head, Dumarest lifted up a knee in a savage blow at the groin.

Had it landed as he intended it would have killed, as it was the knee hit bone as Galbrene twisted, slid up over the stomach to be trapped as again the enclosing arms exerted their pressure. Dumarest sent the other to join it and rode for a moment with both legs doubled, knees resting against Galbrene's stomach and then, with an explosive release of energy, he burst clear and was hurtling backward to land on the sand, to roll, to spring to his feet and dart in again to the attack.

To pause as Galbrene swayed.

A momentary pause made in order to gauge the situation. The man looked dazed, turning vaguely so as to present his blind side towards Dumarest. An advantage only a fool would waste.

"In, Earl! In!"

Dephine's voice, high, shrill and close. During the fight they had moved to where she sat on the lower tier, now leaning forward, both hands extended before her, the fingers pressed together and pointing into the arena. A thing Dumarest noticed before he reached his opponent and sent his hands to do their work, the stiffened edges crashing against vital centres, repeated blows delivered with blinding speed which sent the man slumping to the ground.

"Kill!" screamed Dephine. "Kill him, Earl!"

But there was no need. Galbrene was dead.

Chapter Eleven

———◆◆◆———

The chapel was as he remembered, the gloom dispelled only by the tiny flames of the vigil lights illuminating the broken weapons, small patches of brightness to reveal the sacred things. A custom Dumarest could understand; each man had his sacred thing, something set apart in a special place or carried like a vision in heart or mind. For some it was a scrap of cloth, a gem, a faded image, a tender memory. For himself it was an entire world, his home, Earth.

"Earl?" Navalok rose from where he had been kneeling his face taut in the glimmering light. A face tense with strain and marred by envy. "I saw you fight," he said. "They didn't know I was there but I managed to sneak in and stay out of sight until the battle had commenced. Twice I thought he had you but both times you recovered to gain the final victory." He added, wistfully, "I wish I could fight like that."

"A wise man doesn't need to fight at all," said Dumarest.

"You aren't wearing his badges." The luminous eyes examined the plain tunic. "It is your right to wear them, Earl. They will tell all of your prowess. Didn't they offer you the badges?"

The badges, the gun, some items of personal jewelry which he had taken.

"And the gun," said Navalok. "Why aren't you wearing a gun?"

"I haven't the right."

"But—" The boy paused, frowning. He was troubled at the contradiction; Dumarest had killed an armed adult in fair fight and by the custom all the man owned in the way of personal gear was his as the spoils of victory. And yet he, a proven fighter, carried no gun. No visible and accepted proof of his manhood.

"The gun was proof of Galbrene having won his trophy," said Dumarest. "It was his trophy, not mine. Until I gain my own I have no right to carry a gun. Isn't that the case, Navalok?"

An appeal to his knowledge. An adult talking to him as if he were an equal. A red tide of pleasure rose to suffuse the pale cheeks.

"Technically you are correct, Earl. A small point, perhaps, but one of importance. To defy the custom would be to invite challenges and there could be many who would be eager to prove themselves." He spoke like an old man who has spent too many years breathing the dust of books. "In any event gaining a trophy would be, for you, a mere formality."

Again the envy, the wistful longing, emotions too long repressed and triggered into stinging wakefulness by his sight of the recent combat.

Dumarest said, "How would I go about it?"

"Go into the hills, find an olcept, kill it and return with its head to place before the Shrine." Navalok added, "No guns, of course, only hand-weapons such as a sword, a spear or," he glanced at Dumarest's boot, "a knife."

"Do I need witnesses?"

"Usually a youngster is accompanied by an adult when he sets out to make his kill, but there is no law insisting on it. Just return with a trophy—that will be enough."

A small thing, quickly said and casually mentioned, but Dumarest could sense the fear in the artificially stilted voice, the sick longing which must make the boy's life a hell. To venture out, to kill, to return in triumph.

The dream of one branded as a coward.

Dumarest turned, avoiding the luminous eyes, looking around the chapel. Nothing seemed to have changed but something was missing. Something he had expected to find.

Navalok said, when he mentioned it, "Galbrene isn't here, Earl. He has been taken to the preparation rooms of the Hall of Dreams."

"Is that normal?"

"He died in combat. Before he is laid out for those who wish to pay their homage he must be presented as they remember him. Later he will be taken and set in his place there to sit and dream for eternity."

Dumarest said, "You know these things. Is that how you

spend your time? In studying the traditions and customs of your Family?"

Navalok said, dully, "My father died in the crash which left me with a twisted foot. My grandfather fell to a death-challenge. My mother formed a new alliance and has a younger son. By custom and tradition I should take my place at the Highest Table and don the authority of the House. It is necessary for the one who rules to know the history of the Family and be able to pass judgement on the right of any challenge and any appeal. To be weak is to risk dissension and destructive partisanship. It has happened before when brother fought brother and no man could be sure of who was a friend. So I study in order to be able to pass the tests of fitness and knowledge. Fitness as to determine judgement, of coure, the other—"

Dumarest saw the eyes move to the broken weapons, the lights, the thing they represented. Strength and courage and the visible proof of manhood. He remembered Hendaza's sneer. The boy must gain his trophy soon or be relegated to the lower strata there to be scorned and treated with disdain never to take his high position.

A problem, but not his.

"The preparation rooms," he said. "Where Galbrene is lying. Could I see him?"

An unusual request, he could tell it from the sudden shift of the eyes, the abrupt look of wonder. A man defeated was, by his victor, a man forgotten.

"Yes, Earl, if you want."

"I do. Is it far?"

It was where he should have known it would be, set close to the House, forming an integral part of the structure and now overlaid by a maze of rooms and chambers. The great doors were clear and it was obvious the walls had been extended and would be again in order to accommodate what rested within.

Dumarest followed Navalok as the boy guided him to a room which stank of chemicals. A dimly lit place containing stone slabs set on a stone floor, runnels channelling the flags and leading to a drain. A second chamber held a great vat of noxious liquid in which naked bodies like flensed beasts floated beneath the surface, held down by broad straps weighted with lead.

An old man, armed with a long wooden paddle, stirred the liquid and held up a hand to cup an ear as the boy shouted at him.

"Who? Galbrene? He isn't ready yet."

"I know. Where is he?"

"Waiting presentation. In the annex." The man thrust his paddle irritably into the liquid. "Hasn't a man enough to do without young fools asking stupid questions? Get on your way, now. Move before I splash you!"

Galbrene lay in a smaller room, one scented with floral perfumes and lit by the gentle glow of yellow lamps. He rested supine on a wooden table, a decorated cloth covering his body, his hands crossed over his chest. In the soft lighting he seemed to be asleep.

"Earl?"

"Leave me," said Dumarest.

"But—"

"There is something I must do." And then, with quick invention, "A homage I must make to ease myself of the burden of his anger. It is a custom of my people."

And explanation enough to anyone born into a culture obsessed by tradition and ritual.

As Navalok padded from the room Dumarest leaned forward and studied the body. The damage to the eye had been masked and the nose set straight. The blood, sweat and oil had been washed away and, aside from a slight puffiness of the lips and the dark mottle of bruises on the throat the man looked unharmed.

A jerk and the covering fell away to leave the dead man naked.

Slowly Dumarest inspected him, turning over the body and lifting the arms. He found it beneath the left shoulder-blade, a small, dark-edged puncture, one which could have been made with a heavy bodkin. He leaned close and sniffed at it, pressed the surrounding flesh with his thumbs and sniffed again. A wound too small to have attracted attention and those who had washed and prepared him had no reason to search for anything unusual. Even if they had spotted it it would have meant nothing to them.

Navalok was waiting in the room containing the stone couches. One was occupied now by the body of a young woman, the soft flesh marred by wounds in the stomach and chest.

"The Lady Sepranene," explained Navalok. "They've just brought her in. She challenged the Lady Glabana and wouldn't listen to good advice. She insisted it should be without armor and she had the right."

"To die?"

"To insist. Glabana, so she claimed, was making advances to her lover. The act wasn't denied and after she had publicly accused the woman a challenge was inevitable."

Dumarest said, dryly, "Of course."

Navalok caught the tone and was quick to defend the dead girl.

"She had no choice, Earl. Glabana slapped her face in public. She could have drawn and fired then and the act would have been justified but she adhered to the code."

And died defending a brittle honor. Dumarest looked at the young face wreathed in twisted curls, the lissom lines of the lush figure and his lips thinned at the waste.

Watching him Navalok said, "You don't approve, do you? Is that why you're not wearing Galbrene's badges?"

"There would be no point."

"But—"

"What will happen to her now? The dead girl, I mean."

"She will be cleansed and prepared as Galbrene was prepared. After she has lain in the chapel she will be treated before taking her place in the Hall of Dreams." He glanced to where the old man stirred the fluid in the open vat. "It will take several days."

Time enough for the chemicals to penetrate the tissue, to harden soft fibres and dissolve points of potential corruption. To seal the flesh in a film of plastic, perhaps, or to petrify it, to protect the body against the ravages of time.

To produce monuments to the dead.

They rested in the great hall of the adjoining chamber, massed ranks of them, men and women placed to either side of a central aisle. They faced the external doors, now closed, empty space stretching before them, the plain stone floor fitted with benches to take the anticipated burdens. The bodies of those who would, inevitably, die.

"The Hall of Dreams," whispered Navalok. "Each of them gained his or her trophy which is why there are no children. All died honorably, some of age, most of wounds, but none ever disgraced the Family. Here they sit and dream for eternity."

Lifelike figures who sat and stared with open eyes, the flicker of lights dancing and giving them the appearance of life. Eyes which seemed to follow Dumarest and his guide as he stepped forward between the benches to stand in the central aisle. Curiously he studied the figures to either side.

A man, one elbow resting on his knee, his hands gnarled, the fingers curled, the gleam of a ring bright against the withered flesh.

"A victor," whispered Navalok. "One who later died of his wounds."

Another who leaned back, head a little turned as if listening to a voice from behind. A third who looked as if he might be coughing. A fourth who, with lifted hand, tugged at an ear.

And the women were similar in their staged actions; one smoothing her gown, another picking at a thread, a third who, with pursed lips, gave the appearance of blowing a kiss.

Hundreds of them, thousands, the vastness of the hall was packed with mummified figures.

Dust rose beneath Dumarest's boots as he walked towards the shadowed rear of the hall. The stone of the walls changed its nature, became striated with minerals, grained and mottled with time. The air too held an acrid scent, one of dust and stagnation. Reaching out he touched a figure, caught it as it fell. It was surprisingly light. The clothing it wore crumpled to powder beneath his hand.

"Earl! Be careful!"

Dumarest ignored the admonitory whisper from his companion. He looked from the back of the hall to the figures seated lower down towards the doors. Their clothing had altered little, a static culture froze fashion as it did everything else, but some differences were obvious.

As it was obvious that those who had been placed in the far end of the chamber were old. Old with the crawl of centuries, of millennia.

Navalok gestured to where a small group occupied a raised platform. "The Elders of the First," he whispered. "They are of those who first came to Emijar."

It was natural to whisper, the ranks of silent bodies seemed to be listening, and the atmosphere of the place held a brooding solemnity. Dumarest strode to the platform, stepped onto it, leaned forward with narrowed eyes to study the figures it contained.

The light was bad, dim from suspended globes and dulled with accumulated dust, but it was enough for him to distinguish the motive each wore on their garments; a disc surrounded by tapering spikes.

"What is this?"

Navalok craned his head and followed the finger pointing at the yellow fabric.

"I don't know, Earl. It had something to do with their religion, I think. That device was worn by the Guardians of the Sun."

The sun?

The sun!

Had they known only one?

Dumarest looked at the silent figures, the contours of their faces, the shape of their heads. Compared with Navalok the differences were slight but unmistakable. If priests they may not have married and their genes would have been lost to the common pool. A select group, then, guarding an esoteric secret?

He said, "In your studies, Navalok, did you learn from where the original settlers came?"

"From another planet, Earl. Where else?"

"Its name?"

"I don't know. The records were lost in a fire shortly after the First Families made Emijar their home. In fact nothing is left of them aside from the things in the Shrine and those—"

He broke off as if conscious of having said too much, a fact Dumarest noticed but ignored. Later, if at all, would be the time to press.

"The Shrine, boy," he said. "Take me to the Shrine."

The journey was not long but each step had been taken before many times in other places and, always, such journeys had led to disappointment. A quest which seemed to have no end. A mystery which had yet to be solved. A world lost as if it had never been and yet he knew that it existed and was to be found. Would be found given time and the essential clue. The one fact which would supply the coordinates and guide him back home.

Would fate, this time, be kind?

"Earl?" Navalok was worried at his silence, his expression. "Have I offended you?"

"No."

"If I have it was without intent. No insult was implied in anything I may have done or said. If for any reason you have cause to feel offence then I apologise, humbly and without reservation. Please, Earl. You must believe that."

"I believe it." Dumarest turned to look at the anxious face and smiled. "How could you insult me? We're friends, aren't we?"

"Friends?" Navalok blinked.

"Of course." Dumarest dropped a hand on the boy's shoulder. "Didn't you want for us to be friends?"

"Yes," Navalok stammered. "Oh, yes, Earl. I—I'd like that very much."

A smile and a few words, cheap to give but what seed could bear a richer harvest? Those who took a perverse pleasure in deriding the unfortunate lost more than they knew and risked more than they imagined. No human being, no matter how insignificant, can safely be demeaned. Always there is present the danger of restraints snapping, of self-control giving way beneath the impact of one insult too many. Of pride and the need to be an individual bursting out in a tide of relentless fury.

A thing Dumarest had learned early in life but which Lekhard had not.

He straightened from where he leaned against a wall his voice, like his face, holding a sneer.

"Well, Earl, as I guessed, you find our little freak entertaining. There is, of course, no accounting for tastes, but surely there are others more suited to your whims?" His gesture made his meaning plain. His laughter, devoid of humor, made it obscene.

Dumarest felt the boy tense at his side, the sound of his sharp inhalation, and cursed the unfortunate meeting. To maintain the newly formed friendship he would have to act in a manner which the boy expected which, in this society, meant only one thing.

He said, curtly, "What do you want, Lekhard?"

"I? Nothing, not from you or from any man." Lekhard stressed the gender. "But Dephine was anxious and asked me to look for you. It would be best if you hurried back to your mistress."

Another insult to add to the rest. Dumarest studied the man, saw the way he stood, the way in which his hand rested near the butt of his gun, the expression in his eyes. One he had seen before across countless rings. The look of a man enamored with the desire to kill.

Quietly he said, "Navalok, instruct me. How do I challenge this man?"

"Earl! You carry no gun!"

"Answer my question."

"He has." Lekhard moved from where he stood and halted a few feet from the couple. "Until you have proved yourself you have no right to issue a challenge. The killing of Galbrene makes no difference. It was the act of an animal and I've no intention of following his example and meeting you or any man with bare hands. If you want to challenge me then earn the right to carry a gun. Until then remember your place."

"And that is?"

"In the dirt, scum! In the filth where you belong!"

Dumarest snarled, "I am armed. My knife against your gun. Give the word, boy."

"No, Earl! You—"

"Give it!"

He moved as the youth shouted, wasting no time on snatching the knife from his boot, darting forward and to one side as Lekhard clawed at his gun, closing the distance between them before the weapon lifted free of its holster. His left hand clamped on the wrist, twisting as his right sent fingers to close on the other's throat.

As the gun fell from the nerveless fingers to clatter on the stone of the floor Lekhard sagged, his face mottling, only the hand at his neck preventing him from crumpling to the stone.

Dumarest held him, counting seconds, then threw him to land sprawling against the wall.

"You—" Lekhard rose, coughing, rubbing at his throat. "I'll kill you! My gun—"

"I'll take care of it." Dumarest picked it up and held it casually in his hand. "You can collect it later from the Lady Dephine. I'll tell her you loaned it to me for examination." He added, bleakly, "Or you can tell her the truth as to how I obtained it. Her and everyone else of the Family. The choice is yours."

A choice which was none at all—Lekhard would not want to be shamed by the truth. As he left the chamber Dumarest turned to Navalok and threw him the weapon.

"Here. Take it. Does it make you feel more of a man?"

A mistake which he recognised as the boy caught the pistol. For him to own a gun was to *be* a man, but it had to come in a certain way, one hallowed by tradition.

"I can't take it, Earl. It isn't mine." Reluctantly he handed back the weapon. "But, Earl, the way you faced him! To best him with your bare hands."

A performance which had mainly been for the boy's benefit.

Dumarest said, curtly, "Let's get to the Shrine."

Chapter Twelve

A century earlier and there would have been armed men standing in honor, a guard carefully chosen and each man jealous of the privilege. A generation ago and older men would have tended the sacred place, sitting and dreaming of past glories, of the strength and vitality of their youth. Now there was only a crippled boy to tend the lights and to sweep the dust and venerate the past.

He said, "Earl, this is where the trophies are thrown when the hunters return after having made their kills."

Dumarest looked down at the floor, the place at which he pointed. It lay before the opening of the Shrine, the stone slightly concave with repeated washings. In imagination he tried to visualize the severed heads and the crowd who had watched the ancient heroes. Now there would be no crowd, only an official of some kind to record the achievement. Alorcene, perhaps, or an assistant. And even he would probably have to be summoned.

"Word is sent from the Watcher," explained Navalok when he mentioned it. "Always there are men stationed in the highest tower. They see the immediate surroundings and, of course, word would also be sent from the raft-enclosure."

"And?"

"Men will come to witness the trophy. The notation is made in the records and, later at dinner, the gun is given in ceremony."

A standard weapon each identical aside from personal adornment to the one he had taken from Lekhard. Dumarest examined it, a primitive thing with a revolving chamber holding five cartridges. The calibre was large, the charge, he guessed, small. The bullet would have high impact-shock but

114

low penetration—to be expected in a weapon intended for use in a crowd.

"Earl, would—" Navalok broke off as Dumarest met his eyes.

"What?"

"Nothing." The boy gestured towards the opening. "You wanted to inspect the Shrine."

Not the Shrine but the items it held. Dumarest strode to the slab of polished stone and looked at them. Rubbish for the most part, bits and pieces, some seeming to belong to other, larger artifacts, all showing signs of the ravages of time. Of use and time, the leaves of the plastic file were scuffed a little as well as faded and the metal of the chronometer held a dull patina which covered a worn inscription.

Dumarest rubbed at it with his thumb and held it closer to the light. Narrowing his eyes he read, ... OTA.F TE . .A. The few discernible letters were followed by a disc surrounded with tapering spines—the symbolic image of a sun.

Dumarest lowered the instrument. The words could spell out the name of the ship and place of origin, the symbol would be a general identification device such as even now was used on the multiple commercial space lines. The Songkia-Kwei used the symbol of an open flower—the lotus. The Aihun Line a twisted helix.

Something, a name of—where?

He examined the instrument again, tilting it so as to throw the letters into prominence.

TE. .A

TELLA—No, TERRA?

TERRA!

An alternative name for Earth.

Navalok had been watching. He said, anxiously, "Earl, is anything wrong?"

"No." Dumarest took a deep breath and set down the chronometer. He could be reading too much into too little. The almost obliterated words could have meant something entirely different and, even assuming the last would have been the planet of origin, it need not have been Terra. And yet the chance existed and could not be ignored. "Do you have any more items like these?"

"Not here, Earl. There are Shrines in other Houses as I told you, but they are much the same."

And impossible to visit or examine. Dumarest knew of the jealous pride each Family maintained, the almost fanatical isolation they kept from each other. With time and money, perhaps, it could be done, but he had neither. And it might not be necessary. He remembered the boy's previous hesitation, his obvious reluctance to reveal information. A secret he could be hiding and one Dumarest had to know.

"A pity," he said, casually. "I'm interested in old things. It would be nice to find more of them somewhere. Are you interested in the past?"

Navalok blinked at the suddeness of the question.

"I—yes, Earl. I am."

"The old days," mused Dumarest. "When men landed to settle new worlds. Think of the challenges they had to face. The dangers they had to overcome. Each item of their equipment is a thing of veneration. Every scrap could tell us something new. If you knew where there were more of these things you could become an authority, Navalok. Your fame would spread and learned men come to consult you on their problems."

The wrong approach, the boy was not interested in academic distinction. Dumarest recognised it and said, "The House would be proud of you and you would earn the respect of the entire Family. Women would beg you to father their sons as they did the heroes of old." A shrewd guess but, Dumarest felt, a right one. He ended with a shrug. "Well, it would be nice, but unless such things can be found it must remain only a dream."

To press more would be to press too much, to arouse an antagonism or to wither their new-found friendship. For too long the boy had been rejected, used with cynical contempt, ignored. He had built up a layer of defense and, to threaten it, would be to turn trust into suspicion.

And the information, if he had it, would be a closely held secret.

Dumarest strolled from the opening, his face bland, a man who had seen all there was to see of any interest. As if by accident the gun fell from his pocket to clatter on the floor. He picked it up, turning it, bouncing it on his palm, conscious of the boy watching, the hunger in his eyes.

As he put the weapon out of sight Navalok blurted, "Earl, there is such a place. I know where more of these things are to be found."

Dumarest was deliberately obtuse. "A museum?"

"No. It's in the hills. I found it one day when my father took me out in a raft. I think he was looking for game. We landed and later I went exploring on the slope. I found a cave. The light was bad but I saw things like those." He gestured towards the objects littering the polished slab of the Shrine.

"And?"

"My father said it was an important discovery. He was going to report it but on the way back something went wrong. The raft crashed and he was killed and I—" He looked at his twisted foot. "I didn't say anything."

A child, hurt, bewildered, keeping the discovery to himself for reasons he couldn't have consciously known.

And now?

"I'll guide you if you promise to help me, Earl," he said in a rush. "If you'll teach me how to kill an olcept. If you'll help me to gain my trophy."

Dephine said, her voice edged with anger, "Earl, you're mad! Insane! The thing is ridiculous!"

He said nothing, watching as she paced the room with long strides, her hair a tumbled mane, her skin glistening with a moist warmth. She had just bathed and, as she walked, each step revealed the long, flowing line of her thighs through the slits in her robe.

"You can't do it, Earl!" She halted before him and he could smell the perfume she wore, the slightly sweet odor of decaying blooms. "You can't!"

"Why not?"

"Because it's dangerous, you fool, that's why. Men get killed hunting an olcept, women too, my own sister—well, never mind. But I don't want you hurt or killed, Earl. You mean too much to me for that."

He said, dryly, "Is that why you killed Galbrene?"

"Killed Galbrene?" She frowned. "I didn't kill him, Earl. He fell beneath your hands. Everyone saw it."

"They saw him fall," he corrected. "But I didn't kill him and we both know it. He was dazed when I made the final attack, dying where he stood. Didn't you think I could manage him?"

"Earl, you're wrong. I didn't touch him."

"Why bother to lie?"

"I'm not, Earl. I swear it!"

For a moment he held her eyes then his hands reached out, caught her own, lifted them so the gleaming nails pointed towards the ceiling. Beneath the curve of sharp metal on her right index finger he could see the tiny hole of a surgical implant; a narrow tube which had been buried in the flesh. The finger of her left hand held another. It spat a minute cloud of vapor as he squeezed the first joint, the nodule he discovered beneath the skin. On the ceiling a tiny dart hummed to vanish into the plaster.

An effective range of about ten feet, he decided, more if the target were unclothed. The dart would bury itself within the tissue by ultra-sonic vibration and be coated with a blood-soluble poison.

"An assassin's weapon," he said. "It goes well with the nails."

"One never used before, Earl. You can believe that."

"What difference if it has?"

"None." She rubbed at her hands then stared her defiance. "And what business of yours is it if I did? What I've done before we met is no concern of yours. As what you've done is no concern of mine. For me, Earl, life began when I met you. Real life, I mean, not the shallow searching for adventure that had gone before. I love you, Earl. Don't you understand that? I love you!"

"And you killed Galbrene to prove it?"

"I killed to save you and would do it again if I had to." Turning she swept across the room, knocking against a small table in her agitation, sending a delicate vase to shatter on the floor. "Galbrene had you. I thought he would break your back. The man was like an animal in his strength. Can you honestly say that you could have beaten him on level terms?" She didn't wait for an answer. "It was a chance I daren't take. You had moved close, were within range, all that remained was to make sure I hit the right one. Your attack covered his fall."

And protected her position. If nothing else Dumarest could appreciate the desire to survive which consumed her.

She shrugged as, dryly, he mentioned it.

"So I was thinking of myself a little too, Earl. Can I be blamed for that? You know what would have happened to me had you fallen. But you didn't fall and everything is fine now. So why are we arguing?" Her smile held invitation. "Surely there is something more entertaining we could do?"

The nails, the secret weapons, the smile, the turn of her hips and the sidelong glance, the allure she knew so well how to project. All the hallmarks of the accomplished courtesan and yet, as she had reminded him, what had her past to do with the present?

And, as she had also pointed out, who was he to judge?

"Earl!"

She was close to him, the robe open now, the parting revealing the long, lissom lines of her body, the contours of which he knew so well. Why not just accept her as she was, to ride the tide of seductive passion to whatever shore might be waiting?

"Earl?"

He smiled at her frown and gently reached up to touch the crease between her eyes, smoothing it away with the tips of his fingers.

"Are you going to help me get a raft, Dephine?"

"No! Ask Hendaza."

"I have. He referred me to Kanjuk who, quite politely, referred me to you." Dumarest kept his voice casual. "A matter of traditional privilege, I understand. When I return with a trophy things will be different."

"Earl! No!"

"A small one." His smile widened a little. "The size won't matter. But once I have it I won't have to beg for favors. And," he added, "I won't have to risk being shot for insulting a superior."

"Lekhard?" She glanced to where the man's gun lay on a table. "He never gave you that to simply look at, Earl. There's been trouble between you, hasn't there?" She frowned again as he remained silent. "I don't trust that man. He's dangerous."

"Jealous would be a better word. Is he in love with you?"

"Love?" Her shrug was expressive. "Call it greed, the desire to possess, to own. He wants to prove himself a better man than you are by taking something you own. A fool, but others share his folly. Too many of them are eager to best you in the arena and in bed." She looked thoughtfully at the gun. "Maybe if you carried one of those they would think twice. You're right, Earl, you need a trophy. But you don't have to get it the hard way."

"No," he said. "That's why I need to go into town."

"To buy a gun?" She smiled with quick understanding. "Get it from the trading store run by the Hausi. It's close to the field." Slipping a ring from her finger she handed it to him. "This should fetch enough to buy what you need. I'll authorise the raft, but what of the driver?"

"I can handle it."

"But you'll have to take someone with you."

"I will," he said. "Navalok."

The town was small, a collection of low buildings, a tavern, a hotel for those held on business, the usual warehouses holding goods waiting shipment. The trading store was a large building containing an open room backed by a counter. Leaving the boy in charge of the raft Dumarest went inside.

"Welcome." Telk Yamamaten came forward from an inner room, his eyes shrewd beneath heavy brows. His skin, a dark chocolate, was scarred with the markings of his Guild. "How may I help you?"

Dumarest placed the jewelry he had won on the counter.

"You wish to sell?" The Hausi grunted as he stirred the heap with the tip of a finger. "This is cheap stuff. Flawed gems and coated base-metal. From Galbrene?"

"You know?"

"There isn't much happens on this world that I don't get to hear about, Earl. I may call you that?" He continued as Dumarest nodded. "I knew your name an hour after you'd landed. The fight before the body was cold. Why didn't you take the gun and badges?"

"Would they have been worth anything?"

"The badges, no, but the gun would have brought a little. But you were wise to refuse it. A thing like that can have a big effect on the way they regard you." He added, dryly, "Am I telling you something you hadn't thought of yourself?"

"I'm always willing to learn."

"Now you're being polite. That helps too when it comes to dealing with the Families. They're on the way out, you know. Dying."

"Decadent?"

"Decadent and dying." The agent held up a hand, the fingers splayed. "A Family," he explained. "The Keturah, for example. The name covers the entire genus, the fingers are branches, the Allivarre, the Caldillo, the Pulcher and so on; but all stem from the same root. They won't marry outside their Houses and so they're all inbred to a high degree. The others Families are the same. The only way they can survive is to break the pattern, marry outside their Houses and revitalize the gene pool. It won't happen, of course. Tradition is against it."

Dumarest said, "How much for the jewelry?"

It lay between them, a few rings, a bracelet, a torus of interwoven strands studded with minute gems, a brooch. He added the ring Dephine had given him.

Yamamaten examined it, dropped it on the heap of other items.

"Five fifty rendhals," he said. "That's a little more than the cost of a short High passage."

"Cash?"

"Yes—I can do a little better for trade."

"I want the passage," said Dumarest. "I'll take the rest in kind. On hire if that's possible. You've a ship due soon?"

"The *Ahdil* if it's on schedule. Captain Ying is a friend of mine and I'll arrange a passage. You object to working if necessary? No? Well, maybe I can work something out. Leave it to me." A casual arrangement but a Hausi did not lie and the word of the agent was his bond. "Now, about the other things?" He stared his surprise as Dumarest told him what he wanted. "You going on an expedition or something?"

"I want to explore a cave."

"And camp out?"

"For a few days, yes."

"It's your business, but be careful. The olcept move around quite a bit in the hills and they could be attracted to where you are. I'd advise a heavy-duty laser, expensive, but worth it. No? A gun then, at least. Why beg for trouble?"

"Let me see the gun." It was similar to the one Lekhard had worn. Dumarest spun the chamber and snapped the trigger a few times. Yamamaten shrugged at his expression.

"It's standard to the Families and there's no point in stocking anything else. A holster? Ammunition?" He pursed his lips at the amount. "That's enough to start a war."

"No, just enough to teach someone how to shoot."

"The Lady Dephine? She doesn't need to be taught. She

might be out of practice but, at one time, she could hit a mark with the best of them."

"You knew her?"

"She left shortly after I came to Emijar. That was years ago and I never thought she'd return. Once they get away they stay away—those with the courage to make the break. But she was unusual, full of fire and ready to challenge at the drop of a word. Fast too, so I've heard, and a little vicious. She'd aim to maim rather than to kill."

"Perhaps she was giving the fallen a chance?"

"Maybe, but they didn't look at it like that. Anyway, she's back now so what does it matter? A local girl who made good." The agent smiled and added, dryly, "But you'd know about that."

Dumarest said, "Has she been enquiring about ship-ar-rivals?"

"No. Is there anything else?"

"One thing—how do I kill an olcept?"

"Kill an olcept?" The agent narrowed his eyes, suspecting a joke and ready to be annoyed at the affront to his dignity. Then he said, slowly, "You mean it. Hell, man, you just take a gun and shoot it."

"And without a gun?"

"Of course! You want a trophy! Sorry, Earl, I didn't catch on. Well, the best thing to use is a spear. One with a long blade and checks at its root. You ever seen an olcept? No? Know what they look like? Good. Well, the gripping appendages aren't too serious, they use them to grip at food. In fact—here, let me show you."

He led the way to the back of the store, through a door and into a walled courtyard. Doors lined it behind which rested goods for barter, shipment and trade. In the open compound rested a creature about a foot long.

"That's a young one hatched just a week ago. It'll do nothing but eat and it'll grow while you watch it. In about a month it'll be a yard long and then I'll cut its rations."

Dumarest squatted better to study the olcept. Even though small it looked vicious. The snout turned towards him, deep-set eyes burning, the tail lashing and sending dirt leaping from the ground.

"They eat all the time," said Yamamaten. "And they never stop growing. The rate is constant but, of course, the larger they get the slower they grow. A matter of mass-intake and metabolic conversion, but you aren't interested in the biological data."

"Why do you keep it?"

"As a watch-dog. If anything comes over that wall it won't get away alive. They can be trained given patience and will follow a few simple orders. Just like a dog, in fact. When it gets too big I'll have it shipped to a zoo or set it free in the hills." The agent picked a long, thin wooden rod from a bundle which stood beside the door. "Now remember this. The brain is here." He tapped the creature on the reverse of the sloping skull. It's small and well protected by thick bone. It can't easily be reached from above but if you can get the thing to rear you'll be able to reach it from beneath. Strike up and towards the tail from just behind the hinge of the lower jaw. For a big one you'll need a blade at least two feet long, plenty of thrust and a liking for having the flesh stripped from your bones by the front claws."

"The heart?"

"In the center just behind the front legs." Again the tip of the rod marked the point. "If you want to hit the spine aim here." The agent moved the rod. "The bone is thin and flexible. You can reach the gut from either side just before the back legs. Be careful of the stomach-plates, though, and watch the tail." He grunted as the creature snapped off the end of the rod with a flash of gleaming white teeth. "I don't have to warn you about the jaws."

"Any peculiarities?"

"You've hunted," said Yamamaten. "Not many would think to ask that. Well, they don't like to face the sun so it helps to keep it at your back. They can smell better than they can see so keep to windward. And they can hear better than any other animal I know. Move and they'll hear you, spot your position and move in before you know it. And don't try to run. They can catch a running man before he's covered a score of yards." Smiling he added, with grim humor, "Aside from that they're easy enough to kill."

Chapter Thirteen

———◆——◆——

From where he hung over the side of the raft Navalok shouted, "There, Earl! There—to the right and down!"

From his seat at the controls Dumarest saw a scarred slope dotted with scrub, a patch of shadow and something which could have been the opening of a cave. Cutting the power to the antigrav units he allowed the vehicle to fall and come to rest on the slope below the opening.

"Navalok! Wait!"

The boy ignored the command, springing from the raft to run up the slope towards the opening. Dumarest followed more slowly, eyes searching the terrain, noting each rock and clump of scrub. Predators were rare this high in the hills, but there could be stragglers and even a small olcept was to be treated with respect. Above the sun beat down from the zenith and the sky, a clear azure, stretched cloudless to the horizon. A fine day—the second they had been searching.

"Earl!" Dumarest heard the cry of triumph then the bleak admission of failure which followed. "No. No it isn't the one. It's just a shallow cave like all the others. Earl, I'm sorry."

Dumarest led the way back to the raft, lifted it as the boy climbed in. He set the controls so as to hover twenty feet above the ground.

"Navalok, listen to me. When you left the House with your father you headed north. Right?"

"Yes, Earl, as I told you. We traveled from an hour after dawn until noon when we set down and made camp. We ate and I went wandering over the slopes. It must have been say, two hours after landing, maybe a little more."

"And?"

"That's it, Earl. I found the place and called my father and

124

we examined it and he said we should return to the House without delay. We climbed into the raft and he set the course and—" His voice broke, but he forced himself to continue. "And then we crashed."

"When was that? Late in the afternoon?"

"Yes. It was dusk before they found us. My father was dead and I was hurt. For a long time I didn't know what had happened, just that I kept having dreams of falling. When I was strong enough they told me father was dead." He added, bleakly, "And that I would be a cripple for the rest of my life."

A lie, a simple operation could cure the boy's injured foot, and Dumarest wondered at the stern morality which had prevented it from having been done. The pride of bearing visible wounds, perhaps, or the result of some harsh tradition born in the past. A matter which faded into insignificance beside one of greater importance.

Where was the cave?

The boy had been certain he knew exactly where it was to be found. He's been wrong and had since compounded the error. Now he was searching with a wild, desperate abandon, trusting more to luck than anything else. A fact he must know and Dumarest had waited for him to realise it.

"Let's start from the beginning," he said. "When you headed north at what point did you aim? Your father must have had some guide. A peak, perhaps, or a pass, try to remember." And then, as the boy began to speak he snapped, harshly, "Think, boy! Think! Close your eyes, remember. You are with your father again, just setting out. It is a clear day and the raft is moving towards a certain point. You know what it is. Tell me!"

"The Prime of the Triades, Earl." Navalok opened his eyes. "It's the highest of three peaks and lies a little to the east of true north. But we've checked it."

One peak of several, the boy impatient, claiming to have recognised familiar signs, guiding the raft well to the east of the Prime. Dumarest lifted the vehicle higher and sent it towards the specified point. Before he reached it he sent the raft towards the House, turned, headed towards the peak as if they had come directly from the ancient building.

"There!" Excitement made the boy's voice shrill. "Earl! There!"

"No."

"It is, Earl. It is."

The spot at which he pointed was too steep for anyone to make camp and, despite the shadow of an opening, Dumarest moved away from it. A jutting promontory lay a little to one side and lower down, scrub thick at the edges and a natural spot for a raft to make a landing. From a height of a dozen feet Dumarest examined the stoney dirt, saw the traces of a long dead fire.

"Do others come here?"

"Yes, Earl. It's a favorite place. Often fathers bring out their children for private tuition."

Long hours spent in learning how to handle a gun. A good place for teaching and one Navalok's father would have known. Dumarest landed, checked the area, and leaving the raft moved towards the uprising slope of the hill.

"Left or right, Navalok? Can you remember?" Then as the boy hesitated, he said, "It was past noon. Which way was your shadow? Behind you, before you, to one side?"

"Behind me," said the boy after a moment's thought. "I walked towards the sun. This way, I think." His hand lifted, pointed. "Yes, Earl. This way."

A small boy wandering at random over rock-strewn slopes, his face towards the sun. The light and the bad footing would have kept his head lowered and so narrowed the field of his vision. His father, watching, would have suspected no danger so the path must have been one of relative safety. A section of the hill clear of scrub, then, and one of easy access. And it was in the nature of an agile young boy to climb.

As it was the tendency of a child to exaggerate the size of an opening.

Navalok had been looking for an open cave—what he had found was a narrow vent half-hidden by fallen debris and masked by a mass of scrub.

Looking at it again he said, dubiously, "I'm not sure, Earl. The place I found was larger and more open."

The reason he had missed it before, but Dumarest was no longer trusting the boy's memory. Time would have wrought changes, rock could have fallen and the passage of years would have thickened masking vegetation.

"We'll check it out," he decided. "Navalok, get back to—" He broke off, looking into the sky, seeing the tiny shape sweeping towards them, the outline of an approaching raft.

Dephine had ridden alone. As she settled the vehicle down beside the one Dumarest had used she said, dryly, "Well, Earl, this is something new. I'd never have taken you for a teacher."

Beside him Navalok lifted the pistol, aimed and fired, the echoes of the report rolling from the slopes to die like muted thunder.

"Another miss!" He lowered the gun, his voice echoing his disappointment. "I can't understand it. Back in the House at the range I did better than this. Now I can't seem to hit a thing."

"That's because you're trying too hard," said Dumarest, patiently. "Think of only one thing at a time and make sure you do that thing well. As it is you're trying to draw, aim and fire all in a split second. Forget the speed of the draw. Forget trying to get off a lot of shots quickly. Now reload and try again." Turning to Dephine as she stepped towards him, he said, "Out for a ride?"

"Out looking for you, Earl. How long are you going to stay away from my side?"

"We'll be back tomorrow."

"Why not tonight?" The scent of her perfume filled his nostrils as she rested her hand on his arm. "Why waste time with the boy when you could be with me?"

"Tomorrow." Dumarest frowned as the gun roared and again the boy missed. "I've promised to help him and I keep my word."

"To a cripple?" She recognised her mistake and quickly altered her tone. "I'm sorry—I shouldn't have said that. The poor fool can't help what he is but the traditions of the House are strong. Only the fit deserve to survive and to breed. A woman's instinct, Earl. Beneath the skin we are all alike. We all want the best father we can get for our children. The strongest man we can find to provide."

"There's nothing wrong with Navalok."

"His foot—"

"Can be healed and you know it. All it takes is money."

"And the rest?" She shrugged as the boy fired and again missed. "How long would he last even if he did manage to win his trophy? The first challenge and he would be down. The first argument and he would be dead. You're wasting your time, Earl. He isn't worth it."

"It's my time, Dephine."

"And I am waiting for you, Earl. How long must I wait? I expected you back with your trophy yesterday. We could have been married today. Tomorrow would have seen us in our new home. Am I so repulsive that you prefer the company of a lame boy to what I offer? Must I tell you again that I love you? Earl, damn you, must you torment me?"

A woman in love, pleading, forgetting her pride in the face of a greater need. Standing before him she looked radiant, her hair a flaming glory, her body one of feline grace.

"Tomorrow, Dephine." He needed time in which to search. "Tomorrow."

"And tonight?"

"We'll camp here."

"Not here, Earl. The olcept are on the move and are heading this way. Return to the House and be safe. You promise?" She didn't wait for his answer, confident in his obedience, the power of her attraction. "Tonight, Earl. I'll be waiting."

As her raft lifted Navalok said, "Shall I keep on shooting, Earl?"

"Until you hit the target, yes."

"You didn't want her to see us searching," said the boy shrewdly as he thrust fresh cartridges into the pistol. "That's why you had me shoot, isn't it, Earl? Don't you want her to share our secret?"

As yet they had nothing to share, but the boy had guessed the answer.

Dumarest said, "Look at that point of rock. Keep looking at it and raise the gun. Think of it as a finger which you are pointing to the spot your eyes are fixed on. Concentrate. Don't squeeze the butt too hard. Just close your finger, gently, and don't do it until you feel that you, the gun, is pointing at the target." He grunted as stone chipped a few inches from the point. "Better. Try again."

Fire and keep firing until the sky was clear. In clear air sound traveled a long distance and the woman's ears were sharp. A woman who was determined to get her own way and would do anything to bend him to her will. One who would destroy any clue leading to Earth if she thought it would take him from her side.

As the tiny mote of the raft finally vanished Navalok said, "Enough, Earl?"

"Enough. Now let's go and see what we've found."

The scrub was sturdy, the roots deep, the plants yielding reluctantly as Dumarest tore them free. Loose stone followed, debris rolling down the slope as he cleared the mouth of the narrow vent. It was in the form of a rounded arch, the keystone bearing a worn symbol, a barely discernable disc surrounded with tapering rays. The lower part of the opening was blocked with a mass of gritty soil and shattered stone.

Dumarest tore at it with hands and knife, coughed in a cloud of rising dust, then squinted through the opening. A child could have passed through it with ease. An adult, years ago, with a little wriggling. Fresh falls had piled on old, the roots of the scrub splitting stone to add to the detritus.

"I could get inside, Earl." Navalok thrust himself forward.

"No." Who could tell what might be lurking within. "Help me clear this opening."

Thirty minutes later a path had been cleared for the two of them.

"This is it, Earl," said Navalok as he stared into the thick gloom. "The sun must have been just right when I entered it last. It caught something which gleamed. It was that which attracted me, I remember it now."

"You said the light was bad."

"It was, aside from that one bright place. But I could see what was inside. My father too, Earl, he had no doubt as to the importance of what we'd found. If we wait perhaps the sun will shine inside."

"There's no need to wait," said Dumarest. "I've brought lights."

They were powerful flashlights which threw cones of brilliance into the opening to be reflected back in a dazzling brilliance. Moving the beam Dumarest saw a rounded roof carved with vine-like decorations and set with scraps of crystal in various shapes. The walls too, what he could see of them, were also carved and decorated with strips of red and yellow, amber and green, orange and umber material which held and diffused the light to cast a roseate glow.

Holding back his hand Dumarest said, "Give me the gun."

Reluctantly Navalok parted with it. The weapon at his waist had given him the assurance of a man, without it he felt a child again. He watched as Dumarest checked the load.

"Earl?"

"Wait here. Follow when I call. Stay well back until then. If anything is living in there it may try to break out past me. If it does I don't want you to get hurt."

Navalok said, wonderingly, "Earl, you talk like, like father."

"Maybe I feel like him. Stand back now."

Dirt showered from beneath his knees as Dumarest edged himself up and into the opening. He thrust forward the light in his left hand, the gun ready to fire in his right. It swept up and level as something seemed to move and glare at him, his finger easing its pressure just in time. The light, not the thing had moved and the glare came from a mask not a living face.

Quickly Dumarest scanned the area, sending the beam back into the furthest corner of the cave before focussing it on the mask again. It was an idiot's face, the mouth downturned, the empty eye-holes adding to the vacuity of the general expression. An object which radiated a sadness and an empty despair. Turning towards the opening he saw another, almost its twin aside from the fact that this was a depiction of humor, the mouth upturned, the eyes blank though they were, seeming to hold a secret merriment.

"Earl?" Navalok called from outside. His voice betrayed his anxiety. "Are you all right?"

"Yes. Come and join me." Dumarest handed him the gun as he slid down the heap of debris to stand at his side. "Holster this, I want my hands free. Where is the bright thing you saw before?"

It was set high on the rear wall facing the opening; a large disc set with the familiar rays, the whole a dully gleaming golden color. If the opening were cleared the sun, at certain times, would shine on it and be reflected as if from a mirror.

"The Guardians of the Sun," whispered Navalok. "It's the same symbol they wore on their clothing, Earl. You saw it in the Hall of Dreams. But what does it mean?"

A church, a shrine, a place of worship. A cave in which people gathered to pay homage, to remember. Dumarest swept up his torch and saw the gleaming reflections from the crystal in the ceiling, down and saw the glow of warm and lambent colors from the material set all around. The stars? The dawn and sunset? A place in which to recapture the past, to be at one with something held sacred.

The sun.

Which sun?

He looked at the rayed disc its blank face telling him nothing. At the items set all around; the fragments of machinery, small objects which could have been the personal possessions of those now long dead, the scrolls and books and oddly shaped pieces of metal, plastic and crystal. Above the opening the empty, smiling mask told him nothing. A thing set to mock those who would know more than they should? Another symbol depicting—what? The torch flashed as he moved the beam to study the other mask, the one of inane idiocy, the downturned mouth, tragedy as distinct from comedy. The two faces of a universal coin, laughter backed by tears, happiness by misery, joy by sadness, life by death.

"Earl!" whispered Navalok. "Earl, look at the ceiling!"

Dumarest shifted his eyes and froze, stunned by what he saw.

The winking points of brilliance shining by the reflected light of the torch, points which vanished even as he studied them. Impatiently he moved a little, the points shining clear again as the beam of the flashlight hit and was reflected from the rayed disc.

"Patterns," said Navalok wonderingly. "They make patterns, Earl. But of what?"

Of stars. Of the Zodiac. Of the constellations seen from Earth.

Here, in this place, could lie the clue which would guide him home!

Chapter Fourteen

From where he stood at the far end of the room Navalok said, "Nothing, Earl. I've checked every inch. The walls are solid."

"The floor?"

"The same." The boy sounded tired. "No trapdoors, no loose flags, nothing but solid stone as far as I can tell. There could be something under the debris, but I doubt it." He added, curiously, "What are we looking for, anyway?"

A secret vault or hiding place in which important and valuable data could have been stored. A chance and one Dumarest had to investigate; even a negative result held an answer. The clue, if it existed, must be in the chamber itself and not hidden secretly away.

But where?

He swept the light around the place again. Beyond the opening the sky was growing dark with the onset of dusk and soon it would be night. For hours he had checked each item of the store the place contained, finding nothing which told him more than he already knew. The scraps and pieces, each valuable as a relic or as a fragment of the past, were no more than they appeared.

Votive offerings, perhaps. Things placed in this shrine for safekeeping or as a donation to generations yet to come. Who could fathom the intent of those long dead? Yet some things were plain. The cave for one, a natural structure which had been enlarged and lined with blocks of stone each fused to the other by laser-heat. A place intended to resist the ravages of time. One set in a special fashion so as to catch the rays of the sun which, reflected from the rayed disc, illuminated the ceiling and revealed the pattern of stars.

A pattern he had memorized and one he had seen before.

> *The Ram, the Bull, the Heavenly Twins,*
> *And next the Crab, the Lion shines,*
> *The Virgin and the Scales,*
> *The Scorpion, Archer, and Sea Goat,*
> *The Man that holds the watering pot,*
> *The Fish with shining scales.*

The mnemonic which contained the twelve signs of the Zodiac; the constellations as seen from Earth. A clue he had garnered on Technos, seen again on Shajok, and now it was repeated here. Alone it told him nothing new, but it was proof that, whoever had built this place, had come from or knew of Earth.

"Earl, it's getting dark outside." Navalok shivered. "This place is funny. It gives me the creeps."

The influence of those who once had assembled here sending their emanations across time. Trying to relay a message, perhaps, an answer.

Dumarest shone his torch again on the disc and looked at the glitter of the artificial stars. They were a secondary aspect as were the warm glow of depicted sunsets and dawns as the beam glowed from the strips of material lower down. Something to augment the main purpose of the chamber? It had been built by the Guardians of the Sun and the rayed disc occupied a position of natural prominence.

And, if the depicted constellations were those as seen from Earth, then the sun could only be the planet's primary.

Earth's sun!

Dumarest looked down at his hands and saw their faint trembling. Never before during his long search had he felt so close to success, so certain that it was to be found. If he was correct, and logic said he must be, then the people who had settled Emijar had come from his home world.

"Earl?" Navalok hitched at the gun holstered at his waist. "Are you going to stay here much longer?"

For as long as it took to find the answer.

"Why? Are you getting hungry?"

"Aren't you, Earl?"

"No, but if you want to fix a meal go ahead." The boy had helped all he could and his presence was a distraction. As he headed towards the opening, now a deep purple, Dumarest said, "Be careful, Navalok."

"Of what, Earl?" The boy smiled and touched the gun at his waist. "Anyway, I'm armed."

Alone Dumarest swept the torch around in another examination. Reflected light glowed from the masks, the rayed disc, shone from the ceiling, the walls, warm swathes of color blending with crystalline twinklings. The sun, it had to be the sun, every instinct drove him towards it. Why else should this place have been built in the position it occupied? Why the reflection from the orb transmitted to the depicted stars? Why the name?

Guardians of the Sun.

Guarding what? A memory? A heritage?

The knowledge of how to return?

In the light of the torch the rayed disc seemed to shimmer, little strands of color playing over the surface as if it had been coated with oil. Dumarest stepped closer, tilted his head to stare through narrowed eyes, seeing in the glare a mesh of shallow lines close-set as if part of a refraction grating used to determine a spectrum.

Lowering the torch he stepped back and looked around for something on which to stand.

Then froze as, from outside, came the sound of a young voice shouting, the sudden roar of a gun.

The raft was on the flat promontory, the spark of a fire beside it; small flames which shone bright in the purple dusk. As Dumarest thrust himself through the opening he saw the flash of a gun, heard the rolling echoes of the report.

"Earl!"

Navalok was crouched beside the vehicle, face turned towards the slope, the gun in his hand firing as he shouted. In the flash Dumarest could see a bulk beside a heap of stone, a shape which seemed to flicker, to move. He swung the beam of his flash towards it and saw a dull ochre hide, the gleam of exposed teeth. An olcept, perhaps drawn by the sound of the previous gunfire, now moving in for the kill.

Dumarest shouted, hurled himself down the slope, dirt showering from beneath his boots. The beam of the flash wavered, danced over the raft, the crouching boy, the fire, the ground, the beast which had scented prey.

"The gun, boy! Keep firing!"

The blast alone would shock the sensitive hearing, the flash dazzle the eyes, the whine of bullets perhaps force the thing into caution. An old teaching of those who trained young soliders, the art of covering fire and a distractive barrage based on the principle that, while a man was protecting himself, he couldn't fire back.

An effective means of keeping a human at bay, but the olcept was far from human and obeyed a more primitive law. Dumarest saw it move as he reached the level ground, a flash of teeth, the scrabble of claws and the whine of air as the knobbed tail lashed towards the boy. He fired as it hit close beside him, the side of the raft bending to the impact, the graze of the natural club sending him spinning to lie sprawled on the ground, blood at his temple.

Stunned or dead—in either case he was out of the fight. Dumarest had to face the beast alone and he had nothing but his hands, the flash, and the knife in his boot. No natural advantage but his brain.

As the olcept rushed towards him he sprang to one side, raced to the edge of the promontory and turned, the flashlight in his left hand, the naked blade of the knife poised in his right. The creature had halted at the fire, the long snout questing, the eyes like rubies from the reflected glow. A thing about nine feet long and three high, not a large specimen of its kind but its weight would be at least three times that of a man.

A machine designed to kill, the claws capable of disembowelling at a stroke, the tail able to crush a skull or snap a bone, the teeth set in powerful jaws which could bite a man in half. An animal, armed and armored and, to itself, invincible. One which would be a stranger to the concept of fear. A predator which lived to eat and killed so as to eat to live.

Sparks flew as it lunged over the fire, snout extended, claws ripping at the gritty soil. Dumarest waited poised, aiming the beam of the light into the deep-set eyes. An artificial sun which dazzled the thing and caused it to halt, tail lashing, head turning as it scented the air. A momentary pause but before it could move again Dumarest had sprung forward and to one side, leaping over the compact body and racing towards the raft.

In it were the spears he had bought, the weapons with which the boy would gain his trophy. Long-shafted, with edged and pointed blades, the shaft protected by outcurved crescents of steel, they had been designed to penetrate a tough hide and to block the rush of a stabbed beast. A good weapon if used with skill—useless unless he could get his hands on one before the olcept attacked.

Instinct saved him. Dumarest dropped, rolled, felt the brush of air across his scalp as the tail lashed the spot where he had stood. Turning the beast snapped, teeth gouging the soil where he had lain, the snout moving as, still rolling, he slashed out with the knife and dragged the razor-sharp edge across the flared nostrils. A superficial injury which caused no real damage but which sent a flood of blood dripping from the injured organ. Blood which would blunt the sense of smell.

Rearing, the olcept screamed.

It was a thin, high, shrilling sound, one born of rage and designed to freeze prey into immobility by the grating harmonics. The instinctive reaction of a beast which had been hurt and one which gave Dumarest the chance to climb to his feet.

The flashlight had been knocked from his hand and lay to one side, the beam throwing a cone of brilliance over the ground, one edge touching the side of the raft. A guide to the weapons within, but to try and reach them was to risk too much. To run from the olcept was to invite swift and sudden death.

"Navalok! Can you hear me? Navalok!"

A chance, the boy, if dazed, could be recovering and with the gun he could at least provide a distraction, but he made no answer and Dumarest knew that he was alone. As the olcept rushed he moved, darting backwards, lunging forward, the knife a blur in his hand, the point reaching for the snout, the edge rasping over scales, sliding to cut at the side appendage, to send the severed tissue to the ground.

Like an uncoiling spring the beast spun, tail whining through the air, lashing beneath Dumarest's boots as he jumped high into the air. Landing he threw himself forward, the knife like a sword as it stabbed at the junction of a rear leg with the body, the point reaching the soft portion and burying itself deep in the gut.

A savage stab which freed a shower of blood, a shower which gushed into a flood as, twisting the blade, he jerked it free.

Again the olcept screamed. It reared high on its back legs, turning, tail and snout and talons ripping the air in a circle of rending destruction. Dumarest felt the blow across his chest as, too late, he hurled himself backward. A blow which stripped plastic from the buried mesh as the claws gouged deep.

He landed hard against the side of the raft and threw himself over it, snatching at a spear and lifting it as the creature, vicious with pain, came after him. The long blade stabbed at the jaw, sank into the soft flesh beneath the chin, was torn free as the beast shook its head, stabbed again at the eyes.

Stabbed and hit and sank deep into a socket as the front talons ripped splinters from the shaft, smashing the weapon from Dumarest's hands as, desperately, he jumped from the far side of the raft.

The knife was gone, the spear, the gun lying beside the boy was probably empty. And facing him was a half-blind animal savage with pain and determined to kill. One which paused and, with head cocked, snuffed at the air.

One eye was gone, its sense of smell impaired, only its acute hearing remaining intact. Cautiously Dumarest stooped and, sheltered by the body of the raft, gathered up a handful of stones. Rising he threw one to land beyond the creature. It hit with a harsh rattle and, as the head turned towards it, he threw another with the full force of arm and back and shoulder.

A primitive missile which hurtled through the air as if flung from a sling to hit the remaining eye, to pulp it, to leave the olcept blind.

Dumarest was moving as it reared, screaming. Rounding the raft he snatched up the spear and lunged forward, the blade lifted, extended, the point held at an angle to the ground. As it pricked the underside of the throat he dropped, ramming the butt against the side of his boot, forcing it hard against the ground. The shaft bent as the weight of the creature drove the point up and into its throat, its brain, the weakened shaft snapping as, threshing, it flung itself from side to side.

Releasing his grip on the spear Dumarest threw himself to one side, rolled, climbed to his feet. In the glow of the flashlight he could see the glimmer of his knife and, as the beast turned away from him, he snatched it up. The olcept was badly hurt, perhaps dying, but it could still take revenge. Dirt rose in plumes from beneath its feet as, the shattered spear dragging from beneath its jaw, it spun and twisted in blind agony. Blood sprayed to spatter the raft, the ground, the limp figure of the boy. Another step and it would be on him, claws ripping at the unconscious figure, tearing the flesh as they tore at the ground.

Dumarest shouted, moved, shouted again, drawing the thing towards him, backing, darting in to sting with the knife, to back again until, at the edge of the promontory, he gave a final yell then darted aside as, blindly, the olcept rushed, to fall over the edge, to crash down the sheer slope and pulp itself on the ground far below.

Navalok groaned, stirred, suddenly reared where he lay in the body of the raft.

"Earl! I—Earl!"

"Steady." Dumarest was beside him, one arm thrown comfortingly about his shoulders. "It's all right, Navalok. It's all right."

"The olcept?"

"Dead." Dumarest added, casually, "You killed it."

"I killed it?" The boy echoed his incredulity. "But how? The gun? Did I shoot it?"

"No. You missed each time."

"The light was bad and it came so fast there was no time to aim. I remember it coming for me and then there was a blow and I saw stars and . . . and . . . ?" He frowned, trying to remember. "My foot twisted under me. I remember that. Then—I killed it, you say?"

"Yes."

"But how, Earl? How?"

Dumarest lifted a canteen wet a cloth and held it to the injured temple. The raft hovered thirty feet above the ground and a dozen from the edge of the promontory where the beast had fallen. It was late, the stars bright in the sky, the air still with a sleeping hush.

"Earl?"

"Lie back and relax. Just do as I say." As the boy obeyed Dumarest switched on a flashlight and, in the reflected light of the beam, lifted each eyelid in turn and studied the whites of the boy's eyes. They were clear of bloodclots and the bone at the temple was unbroken. "You were lucky, Navalok. No real damage and nothing but a minor concussion. Can't you remember what happened?"

"Only that I was hit, Earl and that I fell."

"Then you managed to get to your feet again and—" Dumarest broke off, shaking his head. "Are you certain you can't remember killing the olcept?"

"Did I?"

For answer Dumarest lifted the tunic he had removed from the unconscious youth. It was smeared and stained with blood. More blood marked the hands, resting in the quick of the nails, lying thickly on the boots. Traces he had purposely made.

Frowning the boy shook his head. "Earl, I—"

"You were hurt and probably dazed," said Dumarest quickly. "But I had no time to worry about that. The thing came for me after you'd been hit and I had to run. When I turned you had a spear and were moving in to the attack. I yelled out, but you didn't answer, and the next thing I knew you were stabbing at the beast. You got it in the guts and then, as it reared, you managed to get the point under the chin. The shaft snapped then and the olcept charged. It was dying and must have been desperate. Anyway, it went over the edge. You'd collapsed and, at first, I thought you were dead. I guess we were both lucky."

"And you carried me into the raft and lifted?"

"Yes, there could have been others." That, at least, was no lie. "I washed you down as best I could and made you comfortable. You were breathing so all I could do was to wait."

Wait and whisper in the unconscious boy's ear, his voice directed at the subconscious, implanting the suggestion of false memories and bolstering the story he had just been given. Words spoken and reinforced as the lad had turned and muttered prior to waking.

A lie which had given him the proof of manhood he craved.

"You've won your trophy," said Dumarest. "When it's light we'll collect the head. Now I want to get back to the cave."

Nothing had changed. Outside there had been blood and death, pain and violence, but within the chamber silence still held sway and the ghosts of the past thronged close as if to whisper their message.

Dumarest stood at the foot of the dirt blocking the opening, the beam of the flashlight bright as it impacted against the rayed disc of the depicted sun. A symbol which he was certain held more than it seemed.

For a long moment he studied it, hearing the small sounds from outside where Navalok, in the raft, washed the blood from his clothes and body. Happy sounds, the boy was vibrant at his gain, the trophy, the gun he could now wear with authority, the place which soon would be his as a leader of the Family. A happiness Dumarest had given; one he wished he could share.

The sun.

Guardians of the Sun.

The message, if there was one, had to be connected with the symbol dominating the chamber. Again he stepped close to it, seeing the play of light over the surface, the interplay of shimmering colors as the beam was refracted from the grating.

A code? Tiny dots formed to spell out words? An equation of some kind? A set of coordinates? A recording hidden somehow in the disc itself?

Fallen stone lay heaped at the foot of the debris. Dumarest gathered it, formed a pile, mounted to its summit and found his hands still inches below the disc. Heightening the pile he rested the flashlight in the dirt so the beam shone full on the disc, his shadow occluding the light as he climbed. The thing was thick, heavy, held firm against the wall. Lifting the knife from his boot he thrust the point beneath the lower edge and heaved. The tempered blade bent a little but he thought he detected a trace of movement. Lifting the steel he jerked at the side of the disc, felt a resistance, jerked again and went tumbling backwards as, suddenly, like a door the rayed orb swung towards him.

The back was hollowed, ringed with a series of patterns, dots arranged as were the artificial stars. In the centre, held by clips, rested an oblong strip of plastic.

It sprang free as Dumarest tugged at it and he examined it as he stood on the floor of the chamber. An almost opaque strip of material bearing nothing in the way of figures or words. He held it before his eyes and saw only a murky coloration. A scrap of plastic without any possible intrinsic value yet it had been kept in the most sacred place of this shrine.

An object of veneration—but what?

The reflected light was dim and he looked at it again as he

held it before the lens of the flashlight. In the bright illumination the colors became clear, a swathe stretching from red to violet marked with dark lines of varying intensity.

A spectrum?

Dumarest turned the flashlight, his hands quivering a little, conscious of the sudden acceleration of his heart. Placing the strip over the lens he shone the beam on the floor. An adjustment and he corrected the focus a little, not much and the pattern shown was far short of that thrown by a projector, but it was clear enough for him to be certain as to what he had found.

The plastic held the spectroscopic record of a source of illumination and that source could only be a star.

It had to be a star.

A sun.

Each had its own spectrogram and no two were alike. As a thumbprint would identify one man from millions so a spectrogram would identify one star from those that thronged the galaxy. And this pattern, he had no doubt, belonged to the sun which had warmed him as a child.

Sol.

Earth's primary.

He held the clue which could guide him back home.

Chapter Fifteen

There were nooks in the House, small places set in secluded ways, some graced with delicate carvings, others the repository of lichens and vagrant beams of light which threw soft illumination over stone and bench and the worn flags of the floor. The roof too was a series of flat spaces, some edged with crenellations, others flanked with high walls so that for most of the day they were filled with shadow.

Places which were the favorite rendezvous of lovers and to which Dephine was no stranger.

"Look, Earl." She pulled at his arm and led him across worn stone to where a buttress made a private spot in the corner of a scented garden. Massed in pots a profusion of herbs made an enticing aroma, their fronds hanging down over the walls and trailing on the ground. "I used to come here often as a child. There was a bench and I used to sit and scratch at the wall. See?"

The bench had gone but the scratches remained; thin lines drawn with a childish hand; a crude picture of a bearded man, a stylised vessel of space, a verse which held within its stanzas an empty yearning.

"Even then I wanted to get away," she murmured. "To escape. The House was like a cage and I was a bird pining to be free. Well, I did get free—and found the entire galaxy was nothing but a larger cage. Can freedom really exist, Earl? Is there any world on which a person can stand and be subjected to no restraint devised by man? Is there no place devoid of the power of those who are consumed with the desire to rule?"

He said, quietly, "If there is I haven't found it."

"And you've traveled further than most and seen a greater variety of worlds." She pressed close to him, her hand resting on his arm. "And you know how to handle men. Navalok will be your friend for life."

"I did nothing."

"No?" She turned and smiled and let her fingers trace the scars on his tunic, the ripped plastic beneath which the protective mesh shone with a metallic gleam. "You gave a boy his ambition. You took a cripple and turned him into a man. Is that nothing? How many on Emijar would have done as much? To kill and give another your trophy."

"No." Dumarest was firm. "Navalok made the kill."

"Or so you made him believe. And he does believe it, Earl. As do others. They can't conceive of anyone relinquishing a trophy to another when he has yet to gain one for himself." Again her fingers traced the scars on his tunic. "But I know better. You are kind, Earl. Gentle and kind. A boy would do well to have you for his father."

And her for his wife. The implication was clear as was the invitation in her eyes. To marry, to settle down, to rear strong sons and lovely daughters, to grow old and leave his seed to continue his line on this world. To forget his dreams and accept the warm and solid comfort of present reality. To cease his search for Earth and to take what she offered.

Her fingers tightened on his arm. "Earl?"

"Let's go down," he said. "Hendaza will be waiting for us."

The man was happy, seemingly relaxed, his smile coming with quick naturalness as he lifted his hands to touch those of Dephine and her companion.

"Earl, the Family has much to thank you for. I add my own, special gratitude. Navalok is now, at last, a man."

The ceremony was over, the notation made in the records, the youth now proudly bearing a gun at his belt. Dumarest remembered how eyes had followed him as he had struggled beneath the weight of the severed head to hurl it down at the opening of the Shrine. Hendaza had radiated an almost tangible relief and Dumarest guessed that his previous contempt and acidity had been intended as a spur. One now withdrawn and a genuine concern taking its place. Fatherless, the boy had found a mentor. Hendaza would take the place of the missing parent.

Lekhard had been edgy, sneering, turning away as he had met Dumarest's eyes. From him, later, there could be trouble but that was not Dumarest's concern. And Kanjuk, Lekhard's companion, had spoken to him and led the man from the assembly as if he had been a child.

Hendaza shrugged as Dumarest mentioned it.

"Lekhard is too ambitious and would have caused trouble had Navalok delayed obtaining his trophy for much longer. As you may have guessed I tried to spur him to courage in my own way. Now, as a potential Elder of the Family, he will crystalise various loyalties. Kanjuk knows that and will keep his friend in check."

"And if he doesn't?" Dumarest was blunt. "Navalok can't meet a challenge."

"He must if necessary." Hendaza was equally blunt. "That is the price he pays for being accepted as a man. But if Lekhard should challenge him without just cause he will face, not just one young man, but a line of others each of whom will challenge him in turn. Eventually he will fall. This he knows."

A mad dog taken care of in the traditional manner, Dumarest could appreciate how it would be done. Other Houses he had known would have called on the aide of assassins, here on Emijar they were more honest—or naive.

"And you, Earl?" Hendaza glanced towards Dephine. "When are we to celebrate your obtaining a trophy? Soon, I hope?"

"Perhaps."

"It will be soon, Hendaza," said Dephine firmly. "He would have had it by now but he had no wish to spoil Navalok's moment of triumph."

"A commendable attitude and one worthy of a man of proven courage. You should be proud, Dephine."

"I am." She smiled with possessive affection. "Very proud. Earl—" The smile changed to a frown as he moved away. "Earl!"

He said, without turning, "I'm going to see Navalok."

The boy was at practice. He stood at one end of a firing range, facing targets shaped in the image of a man, the gun in his hand lifting, to steady, to fire. A light set behind the targets showed where the bullets had struck.

"I'm getting better, Earl. I can hit a man each time I fire now."

"You can hit a target," corrected Dumarest. "A target can't shoot back."

"Neither can a man if he's dead." Navalok lowered the gun, reloaded it, slipped it into his belt. "Watch this, Earl!"

He was a boy, proud of his skill, a child eager to demonstrate his ability. The gun lifted from the holster, levelled, fired. On the target a light shone through a hole in the forehead.

"There!"

Dumarest said, dispassionately, "Navalok, you're a fool. Why aim for the head when the body offers a better target? And what if your opponent is wearing armor? If you want to play this stupid game then do it properly."

"Stupid?"

"If you want to kill a man then do it. Get in hard and fast and, above all, get in first. Don't give him a chance. To do that is to invite death. Don't waste time in talk. Just act and get it done with."

"But Earl, the code—"

"Is a game. Why else do you wear armor at times? To fight and not get hurt—so why fight at all. Now listen to me. Lekhard is no friend of yours and will challenge as soon as he can. How will he do it? Insult you?" Dumarest thinned his lips as the boy nodded. "Right, when he does make sure that witnessess overhear. Be polite and above all don't lose your temper. Look at him as you would vermin. Refuse to be pushed and he will try harder and then, when you've enough provocation, draw out that gun and kill him."

"In public?" Navalok looked startled. "But, Earl, a challenge has to be met with due formality."

"Just kill him," snapped Dumarest. "And argue about it later. Let Alorcene check his records for precedents. He will find them. No society could have grown as yours has without men killing others at the slightest provocation. Restore some of the old traditions—and watch how the challenges suddenly lose their appeal."

"Face him in public," murmured the boy. "Warn him first and then—"

"You don't give any warnings," snapped Dumarest impatiently. "He isn't a friend. He isn't anything but an animal you have to kill before he kills you. So kill him." He added, more gently, "You'll only have to do it once, Navalok. Just let the others see that you don't intend to play their game according to their rules and you might have a chance. It's your life, remember. Don't throw it away."

"I won't, Earl. I'll do as you say—if I can."

He would try and either success or the dead-weight of accepted custom would lead to his death, but Dumarest had done his best and could do no more. Now it was the turn of the other to give.

"I need a raft, Navalok. Can you get me one?"

"No, Earl, you need—"

"An accepted member of the House." Dumarest was sharp. "You have the right, now, and I want to go to town. Will you take me?"

They left as dusk softened the outlines of the hills and early stars began to glimmer in the skies. The boy was silent, sitting hunched and thoughtful beside Dumarest as he sent the raft skimming low and straight towards the field. It was empty of vessels as he'd known and, setting down the raft, Dumarest dropped over the side.

"Thank you, Navalok."

"Shall I wait for you, Earl?"

"No."

"You're spending the night here?" The boy looked at the deserted streets, the sombre bulk of shadowed buildings. All were dark aside from the hotel from which came glimmers of light and the sound of thin, reedy music. "Earl?"

Dumarest said, "Take the raft back to the House. Goodbye, Navalok."

He walked to the hotel without looking back, thrusting open the door and stepping into a long, narrow room. It was almost empty, a scatter of men wearing various liveries sitting at small, round tables. At the far end a staircase rose to the upper rooms. On a low dais an old man blew into a bagged flute his gnarled fingers caressing a series of holes.

"Your pleasure, sir?" A squat man wearing a greasy tunic had stepped from behind a low counter. "My House is honored. Some wine?"

"You have rooms?"

"The choice of a score. Always it is the same until a ship arrives. But first, some wine?"

It was rough, holding the tang of smoke and metal, too acid for his taste and a fitting accompaniment to the music.

As he refilled the glass the squat man said, "A vessel should be calling here soon. The *Ahdil* is about due and, naturally, there could be others. A matter of days only, but waiting can be tedious if only for a single night, so if you'd rather not be alone?"

His glance as he posed the question was suggestive.

"No," said Dumarest. "All I want is a room."

It was small, cramped, the bed sagging, the floor of bare, unpolished wood, but it was cheap and would serve. During the night Dephine came to join him.

She entered like a ghost to stand by the door, looking at Dumarest who, roused by the creak of wood, had risen and was facing her, the naked blade of the knife in his hand glimmering in the starlight coming through the narrow window.

He said, quietly, "Why are you here?"

"Can't you guess, Earl?"

"Navalok—"

"Told me. He had no choice. He is waiting below with the raft."

"You shouldn't have come. Your reputation—"

"To hell with that!" Long legs carried her over the space between them. "Do you suppose I care what others think? My life is with you, Earl. With you—not those worshippers of tradition. Couldn't you smell the dust in the House? Feel the cobwebs brush against your face in the passages and halls? The past dominates everything they do, but I live for the present. I long for the future. Our future, my darling. Ours!"

She moved a little and illusion transformed her; the robe she wore gleaming with the whiteness of a shroud, the mane of hair, bleached by the starlight, turning to silver, even the hollow contours of her cheeks taking on an elfin quality, a delicacy which collapsed time and space and made a fragment of the past suddenly real.

Derai!

But she was long gone, long dead, lost on a lonely world, dust now, all her beauty spent. As others were lost and with them their dreams of happiness. As Kalin was lost.

But, always, the search for Earth remained.

Dumarest looked at the knife in his hand. As he put it down Dephine said, flatly, "You came here to wait for a ship. You want to leave. But why, Earl? Why?"

"This isn't my world, Dephine."

"And not really mine, now. But we could be happy here.

There is a place I know, one I used to visit as a child. There is a lake and a house and we could be alone. Alone and happy, Earl, that I promise you. I would be everything to you—give you all any man could ever need."

A lamp stood on a low table against the wall. Dumarest lit it and watched as the flame crawled up the wick to fill the room with a warm and yellow light. One which banished the illusions as if there had been ghosts running before the newly risen sun. Auburn hair, not silver; an embroidered robe, not a shroud; a strongly determined face; not the childish weakness of the one he had known. Not Derai and, aside from the slight resemblance of the hair, not Kalin.

"I saved your life, Earl," said Dephine softly. "Have you forgotten that?"

"No."

"And you owe me something. There are cultures in which once a man admits to this his life is no longer his. It belongs to the one who has saved it."

"And there are others which holds that if a man saves the life of another he is responsible for whatever that man later does." Dumarest shrugged. "Take your pick, Dephine, which do you choose?"

"Neither—and don't make me feel so ashamed, Earl. Do you think it easy for me to plead? I am a Keturah and we have our pride. But I need you. I can't let you go. You just can't walk away and leave me." Her voice grew a little ragged. "You spoke of reputation—well, consider it. Don't shame me before my Family. They think we plan to get married. At least go through the ceremony and give me the respect they hold so important. What would it matter to you? A few days, a couple of weeks at the most. Earl—would it be so hard?"

She stepped close before he could answer, her arms circling his neck, the warmth of her body a fever beneath her clothing.

"Please, darling." Her voice was a seductive murmur; music to enhance the scent of her hair, the perfume of her flesh. "You are too kind to be so cruel as to leave me so soon. Give me a little time and then, if you want, we can leave together. There will be money and we can travel in luxury. You and I as one, darling, together for as long as you want. For as long as you need me. And you do need me, Earl. You need me as I need you. My love! Oh, my love!"

Chapter Sixteen

Dawn broke with a light wind and gusting rain, chill drops which clung to the window and dressed the panes with pearls. Dumarest rose and looked down at the sleeping woman. Sprawled on the bed, her hair spread in an auburn cloud on the pillow, the long, lissom lines of her figure relaxed in satiation, she looked older than when awake and dressed. A maturity which had little to do with the passage of years. More than time had impressed the tiny mesh of lines at the corner of each eye, the slight pucker of flesh running from nose to mouth, the hardness of the jaw and brows.

Then her eyes opened and, suddenly, the face was no longer a bitter mask but that of a vibrant and lovely woman.

"Earl!" She stretched, arching her body, hands lifted, nails gleaming in the early morning light. "I had such pleasant dreams. We were married and we had a child, a son who looked just like you. We'd gone on a picnic and an animal came towards us and we all rode on its back into a field full of tall grass and wonderful flowers. Do dreams mean anything, darling? I knew a woman once who swore they did. To her a bad dream meant a bad day and when she had one she'd write it all down on a piece of paper covered with inscribed charms and burn it. She'd do that before receiving—well, before starting her day."

"And did it work?"

"Who knows? She was young and to the young all things are forgiven." She stretched again and he could see the neat row of bone where her rib-cage showed beneath the taut skin. Ridges broken only by the mounds of her breasts. A lithe figure, one suited to hardship, but one he was sure which had been cossetted in youth. "Did you dream, Earl?"

149

"A little." A lie, he had lain wakeful through the night.

"Nice dreams?"

"Until they were broken. A ship landed an hour before dawn."

"A ship?" For a moment she stared blankly at him and then, abruptly, surged upright. "A ship? From where?"

"I don't know," he said patiently. "I haven't been out yet. All I know is that a ship landed and is now standing on the field. And what does it matter where it came from?"

"As long as it will take you away from Emijar?"

"Yes."

"You say that!" Her eyes widened to show a rim of white around each iris. "After what we've been to each other! What you promised! Earl, I love you. You can't leave me now. You can't. Not after last night."

A woman's illogic, they had been lovers since leaving Shallah—why should the present incident carry such importance?

He said, quietly, "I'm not going to argue with you, Dephine. We both know what I promised. Anyway, why be upset? All I want to do is to take a look at the ship."

"Is that why you're up and dressed? Earl! You can't leave me! I won't let you!"

He backed as she lunged towards him, feeling the touch and scrape of her metal nails on his face, the impact too light to have broken the skin. His own hand lifted, came down to slap her cheek.

"Keep those damned nails to yourself! I warned you what I'd do if you used them against me again!"

"Earl, I'm sorry!" Tears filled her eyes, falling as she turned to splash against her naked thighs. "I couldn't help it. It's just that the very thought of losing you makes me desperate. Please try to understand. I'm in love with you. For God's sake, man, don't you realize what that means?"

Sweetness and pain, the ineffable joy of affection and the haunting fear of loss. The vulnerability of total surrender. The willing discarding of all defenses and the embracing of the unknown. How easy to hurt a creature who loves. A word, a sneer, a curt gesture, a momentary indifference. How easy to suffer anguish.

How quickly to lose the paradise of the mind and senses.

He said, thickly, "Yes, Dephine, I know what it means."

"Then you forgive me?"

"I forgive you. Get up and get dressed and join me below. If I'm not there wait for me."

"You'll wait for me? You promise?"

"The ship won't be leaving yet," he reminded her. "And if Navalok's still waiting he'll be hungry."

The boy sat in the lower room, his face peaked, his lips blue as he hunched before a smoking fire. A devoted attendant who had spent the night in the raft, entering the hotel only at dawn.

"I saw the ship land, Earl," he said. "The raft is ready if you want to use it."

"I won't."

"But—" His eyes moved towards the stairs. "I thought that you and the Lady Dephine would be traveling back to the House."

"Before you go anywhere you need to eat." Dumarest went in search of the owner and gave him instructions. To Navalok he said, "I've ordered food to be served. When Dephine comes down have her eat breakfast. Have a good meal now."

He left the boy hugging a steaming mug of tisane, stepping outside and feeling the chill drive of rain. The ship rested on the field, a twin to the one which had brought him to Emijar. The port was open and the ramp was down but there were no signs of anyone loading. The rain could have delayed the discharge of any cargo the ship may have carried and it was too early for workers to be at the warehouses.

"Earl!" Dephine called from the door of the hotel. "Earl, wait for me!"

Dumarest slowed and waited until she joined him. The rain dusted her hair with glittering gems. Together they walked to the trading post where the agent, more than anyone, would have information on the vessel. Early though it was he had risen and was hard at work. A sheaf of papers rested before him on the counter and a man wearing a captain's uniform sat drinking coffee at his side.

"Earl! A moment." Yamamaten finished checking the list. "This seems to be in order, Captain. I've a small consignment of hides, some selected grain and a variety of woven material for you. Little profit, I'm afraid, but it should cover your expenses." His eyes flickered towards Dumarest. "And a passenger if the price is right."

The captain grunted, "Stop your haggling, Telk. You know my price."

"I know what you ask, Captain, but that isn't always what you get. Earl, meet Captain Ying. Captain, your passenger if we can settle a price."

Dumarest met the cold stare of a man who had the eyes of a snake. The face matched, thin, wedge-shaped, the lips little more than a gash.. A hard man plying a hard trade.

"So you want to ride with me," he said. "Is Telk holding your money?"

"Yes."

"Then we can settle a price. Be at the field at sunset."

"Sunset!" Dumarest turned as he heard the exclamation. Dephine lifted a hand to her lips and forced a smile. "So soon?"

"Why wait?" Ying gave a frosty smile. "There's no profit in hugging dirt." He added, thinking he knew the reason for her concern, "If it's too soon there's another ship heading this way. It would have been here before me if its generator hadn't broken down. It had to put in at Orteja for repairs. Maybe you could get a passage on that."

"No," said Dumarest. "I'll ride with you, Captain. I'll be at the field at sunset."

A good looking woman, thought the captain as they left the trading post. Any man would be reluctant to leave a woman like that though the reluctance had been on her side, not his. And they had the entire day to do what they wanted though, from the look of her, there was little they had left undone.

He said so and the agent smiled and settled down to discussing the price knowing that agreement was certain but enjoying the opportunity to haggle.

As they left the building Dephine said, "So you meant it, Earl. You're going."

"Yes."

"And if I wanted to come with you?"

He said, "You have until sunset to arrange it. I can't pay for your passage. I haven't any money."

"Then how—" She broke off. "Of course, Galbrene's personal jewelry. I should have known." Halting she turned to look at him, tilting back her head, the gesture revealing the long column of her throat. The rising sun caught her hair and turned it into lambent copper; a halo graced with dying rainbows from the droplets of rain still clinging to the strands. "Earl!"

She was lovely and she knew it. A superbly built woman with a face matching her nature. One who would be at the side of the man of her choice no matter where he might choose to go.

Dumarest said, flatly, "Dephine, I have to go."

"To search for your world," she said, fiercely. "To risk your life a thousand times in order to chase a legend. All right, Earl, Earth exists, I won't argue, but even if you find it will you have found more than you're throwing away at this moment?"

"I don't know."

"But you must look." Smiling she shook her head, a mother gently chiding a child, a wife, the eccentricities of her man. "I'm not good at saying goodbye, Earl. Even now I can't quite believe that you are going to leave me. It doesn't seem possible that we shall never see each other again. But one thing before you go. Please."

He could afford to be patient. "What?"

"Let us have a picnic. One in the place I spoke to you about where there is a lake and a house and the land is kind. It will be like living my dream. A few hours of happiness, Earl. Something for me to remember when you are gone."

Navalok handled the raft, sending it high into the clear air. The rain had ceased shortly after dawn and the sun now blazed with a comforting warmth. The breakfast had been good and his passengers seemed to be in harmony. Food and wine had been packed in a hamper and it promised to be an excellent day.

Looking at the youth Dephine said, "Return in a few years, Earl, and maybe you'll see a boy you'll recognise. One who will look like you and whom I will teach never to be afraid."

"Are you telling me you're pregnant?"

"Would you believe me if I did?" She smiled at him, her eyes enigmatic. "And could you ever be sure that I wasn't telling the truth?" Then, before he could answer, she leaned forward and said, "To the right, Navalok, through that pass and then to the left. The house is in a hollow about a mile beyond."

It sat like a gem in an emerald surrounding, a place of facetted stone and a gabled roof with upswept eaves and windows which looked like smiling eyes. The lake was a mirror edged with reeds, bright with floating blooms. Birds flashed among them like streaks of painted wind and, in the limpid depths, fish sported with an agile grace.

A haven. A place to rest and relax as the sun rose in the sky and the heat increased to still the air and cast a brooding stillness over the area.

Dumarest refused to swim, watching as Dephine dived and swum and climbed from the water to shed droplets in glinting showers as she shook the mane of her hair. Dressed, she sat beside him as Navalok ran with youthful energy beyond the house to inspect the garden of shrubs and scented plants.

"You like it, Earl?"

"Yes."

"It could be yours. All of it."

He said, dryly, "And the price?"

"To love me, Earl. Simply that. To love me enough to want to stay."

A temptation, and she had been right, what more could he hope to find than what was here? But the choice was not that easy.

And then, casually, she said, "To love me as much as you once loved Kalin."

Frowning he said, "Kalin? I don't understand."

"No?" She turned to face him, her eyes pools of secret amusement. "I think that you do, Earl. Kalin was very close to you, wasn't she? A woman who loved you so much that she—well, does it matter now? But I know about her, Earl. I *know!*"

The nightmare in the *Varden* when he had lain sick. The delirium. Dumarest remembered that mind-aching time, the face he had seen haloed with light, red hair which had woken a fragment of the past.

She had probed as he had guessed, driven by nothing more perhaps than a woman's curiosity, but from his answers she had learned.

How much?

"You are a man with a past, Earl," she continued smoothly. "Kan Lofoten hinted as much when I asked him how he could trust you. He mentioned information he held about a certain organisation who would pay highly to get you into their hands. Very highly, Earl."

"And you are greedy, Dephine. Well, what animal is not?"

He saw the look in her eyes, the recoil as if he had slapped her in the face.

"You're a clever actress," he said, bitterly, "but you followed a trade which taught you how to manipulate men. All the protestations of love, the passion, the promises, the bribes. Even to the extent of hinting that you carry my child in your womb. All for what, Dephine? To make sure that I would remain in one place? That I would be available when the Cyclan came to collect me?"

"You knew! You bastard, you *knew!*"

"No." He looked at a face which had grown ugly. "I only suspected. Your concern and sudden need of me. To be your champion, you said, but why come to Emijar at all? You hate the place and were far from popular when you left. So why risk your prize? Why else but to make sure I would be at a predetermined place?"

From behind the house Navalok called, his voice high, his words indistinguishable.

"A clever plan, Dephine. You learned of my value to the Cyclan when I was ill. Did you contact them while I was under treatment on Shallah? Did they tell you exactly what to do or did you promise they would find me in your keeping here on Emijar? The latter, I think. You would want to retain control. A mistake. I thank you for it."

"You—"

"I saw your face when the Captain told us of the damaged vessel," said Dumarest. "The one which had to put in for repair. It would have been here yesterday aside from that. Does it carry a cyber? More than one? Your reward? How much did they promise you, Dephine? No matter how much it wasn't enough."

He saw the flicker of her eyes, the change of expression which told him all he needed to know. Even in delirium he had retained the secret of the affinity twin. She didn't know the arrangement of the sequence-chain—if she had he would have been left with no choice.

Rising he shouted to the boy. "Navalok—take me back to town."

Dephine said only one word. "Lekhard!"

He came from the interior of the house, smiling, a gun levelled in his hand. A man who glowed with the desire to kill, to wipe out imagined insults in a bath of blood.

He said, tautly, "You took my gun away from me once—now try to do it again."

"Lekhard! No! He must be kept alive!" Dephine rose to approach the man, to stand beside him, one hand caressing his arm. "He means a fortune to us, darling. And nothing you could do to him would be worse than what is waiting. If he tries to move shoot at his legs. Smash his knees and leave him to scream his throat raw with pain, but don't kill him."

"I want to kill him. He has touched you. Looked at you as if you were his own."

"I suffered it for your sake, my dearest. So that we could both be rich. If you can imagine how I felt after such filth had touched me you would wonder how I could do such a thing. And when he spoke of marriage! I, a daughter of the Keturah, married to a thing like that! Later, my dear, we shall laugh about it."

Dumarest didn't look at the woman and paid no attention to what she was saying. All his concentration was on the man. Lekhard was like a bomb balanced on a razor-edge—a word, a look, and he would explode in a burst of insane destruction. Even to warn the woman about his state was to invite a burst of missiles. Bullets which, at this range and with his experience, could not miss.

And then Navalok, answering his summons, came running from the back of the house.

The woman saw him, the man, both turning as he skidded to a halt. A fraction of time in which their attention was taken from Dumarest. A split second in which he acted.

His knee rose to meet the questing hand, the knife lifting as his foot fell, the hand lifting to swing forward with the full power of arm, back and shoulder. A move which Lekhard spotted from the corner of his eye. One which spun him back to face Dumarest, his hand lifting, the finger tightening on the trigger. To fall back as the knife slammed into his throat, to send blood gushing from his mouth in a crimson stream.

Dying he fired.

The blade had severed his larnyx, thrust into the neck to reach the spine, to kill as surely as a bullet in the brain. But his finger had been closing, the muscles tense, the death-convulsion enough to complete the action. The gun roared, flame stabbing from the muzzle, the bullet riding a blast of expanding gases to catch Dephine in the chest, to bury itself in her lungs, the heavy ball creating havoc among the delicate tissues.

"Earl!"

Dumarest caught her as she fell, blood running from her mouth, one hand clawing at her waist to fall empty from her holster.

"Earl, I—" She coughed and sprayed his face with blood. "You win, you bastard," she whispered. "You win. You lucky—"

Luck which had ruined the generator of the Cyclan vessel and delayed it long enough for him to escape. Which had led him to say just enough while in delirium for the woman to have seared her flesh in a desperate effort to save his life. Which had caused Navalok to create the distraction which had given him the opportunity to kill.

Now he watched, wide-eyed, as Dumarest gently laid the dead woman on the ground.

"She was beautiful," he said softly. "And she loved you."

Dumarest closed the staring, now empty green eyes.

"Earl?"

"Take me to town, boy. Just take me to town."

To the ship which was waiting. To the suns and stars of the galaxy. To the worlds which teemed in the empty spaces, where it was possible to forget.

DAWsf
BOOKS

Lin Carter's bestselling series!

☐ **UNDER THE GREEN STAR.** A marvel adventure in the grand tradition of Burroughs and Merritt. Book I.
(#UY1185—$1.25)

☐ **WHEN THE GREEN STAR CALLS.** Beyond Mars shines the beacon of exotic adventure. Book II. (#UY1267—$1.25)

☐ **BY THE LIGHT OF THE GREEN STAR.** Lost amid the giant trees, nothing daunted his search for his princess and her crown. Book III.
(#UY1268—$1.25)

☐ **AS THE GREEN STAR RISES.** Adrift on the uncharted sea of a nameless world, hope still burned bright. Book IV.
(#UY1156—$1.25)

☐ **IN THE GREEN STAR'S GLOW.** The grand climax of an adventure amid monsters and marvels of a far-off world. Book V.
(#UY1216—$1.25)

DAW BOOKS are represented by the publishers of Signet and Mentor Books, THE NEW AMERICAN LIBRARY, INC.

BOOKS